RATS SAW GOD

ROB THOMAS

ALADDIN PAPERBACKS

Acknowledgments

Thanks to all my students who have allowed me to continue thinking like a teenager. Thanks to my agent, Jennifer Robinson, of PMA Literary and Film Management, for thinking this book was worth her breaking into the young adult market. To my editor and his assistant at Simon & Schuster Books for Young Readers, David Gale and Michele McCarthy—I appreciate your talent, speed, flexibility, and willingness to talk to me for too long and at all hours. Thanks are also due to my friends, particularly Greg McCormack and Robert Young, who read the manuscript and offered suggestions and encouragement. Thanks to my former student James Dawson for the use of his sports column. Most of all, thanks to my friend Russell Smith for teaching me how to write.

First Aladdin Paperbacks edition June 1996
Copyright © 1996 by Rob Thomas

Aladdin Paperbacks
An imprint of Simon & Schuster
Children's Publishing Division
1230 Avenue of the Americas
New York, NY 10020

Also available in a Simon & Schuster Books for Young Readers hardcover edition.
Book design by Anahid Hamparian
The text of this book is set in 10-Point Industria and 10-Point Gill Sans.
Hand-lettering by Chris Raschka
Printed and bound in the United States of America
10 9 8 7 6 5 4 3 2 1

Library of Congress Cataloging-in-Publication Data
The hardcover edition was cataloged as follows: Thomas, Rob.
Rats saw God / Rob Thomas.
p.   cm.
Summary: In hopes of graduating, Steve York agrees to complete a hundred-page writing assignment which helps him to sort out his relationship with his famous astronaut father and the events that changed him from promising student to troubled teen.
[1. Fathers and sons—Fiction. 2. High schools—Fiction. 3. Schools—Fiction.
4. Divorce—Fiction.] I. Title.
PZ7.T36935Rat 1996   [Fic]—dc20   95-43548   CIP AC
ISBN 0-689-80207-2 (hc)   ISBN 0-689-80777-5(pbk)

To Mom and Pop—
for appearing interested
in every cornball thing I've done.
—R. T.

Though I tried to clear my head of the effects of the fat, resiny doobie I'd polished off an hour before, things were still fuzzy as I stumbled into senior counselor Jeff DeMouy's office. I had learned the hard way that Mrs. Schmidt, my physics teacher, was less naive than her Laura Ashley wardrobe suggested. I made the mistake of arriving in her class sporting quarter-sized pupils and a British Sterling–drenched blue jean jacket. In a random sweep of her classroom, she paused at my desk, sniffed, ordered me to remove my sunglasses, then filled out the forms necessary to land me here.

Wakefield High's powers that be, having exhausted all other options in their losing war against us stoners (including locker-by-locker searches, drug-sniffing dogs, and *Untouchables*-style police raids), were now playing hardball. By order of the principal, I was shuffled off to DeMouy, a UC Berkeley product reputed to be an earth goddess–worshipping, bee pollen–eating, swimming-with-the-dolphins New Age flake. I braced for descent into a touchy-feely hell presided over by a lisping sage who would suggest I give myself a big hug. "Go ahead," I could already hear him saying. "You deserve your share of happiness."

To DeMouy's credit, his office contained no posters of grumpy bulldogs or gorillas with "I hate Mondays" slogans on them. In this respect he had already exceeded the expectations I had for most educators. His office had more of a comfy, oolong-scented seventies feel: lots of plants and a humidifier purring away on top of a file cabinet. One of those environmental sound-effects recordings was evidently being played; I could make out the sounds of waves breaking on the beach, and we were a good three miles from the ocean. All in all, a grand spot to ride out the rest of my high. Through my pleasant dizziness and a potted cactus on his desk, I could see only the back of a manila folder labeled YORK, STEVEN R.

"Tea, Mr. York?" DeMouy asked as he lowered the folder. "It might help you come down a bit."

DeMouy looked nothing like I had imagined from the reports I had received from my brethren. *This* was our new hippie counselor? Surfer confidant? The man before me wore a woolly, regimental-striped tie with a teed-up golf ball monogram.

"No," I said, trying to look impatient. "Just put me in detention. I'll try to get in touch with my feelings there."

"Humor me for a few minutes."

"Okeydokey," I said, slouching a bit further down in my chair and staring unmistakably at the clock above him. DeMouy sipped an obscure Asian blend from a Far Side mug and read from my folder.

"You don't much care for school, do you?"

I deadpanned concern. "Is it obvious?"

"Well, let's see here," he said, thumbing through my portfolio. "In less than a semester you've tallied one *in possession* and three *under the influences*. This is doubly impressive when one considers the nine days of class you've missed . . . ostensibly for health reasons."

He paused to see if I had a reaction. I didn't.

"And then there are the comments on your report card: 'lacks motivation,' 'doesn't turn in homework,' 'falls asleep in class.' "

"Look, this is helping me out quite a bit, but could you just get to the punishment part? We're at the end of World

War Two in history, and I can't wait to find out who wins."

DeMouy shook his head. "You're not in my office because you're high, Steve. For that they just keep sticking you in detention until you see the error of your ways. What I'm interested in is how *this* is possible."

He threw an envelope across his desk. I eyed it cautiously.

"Read it."

The letter was addressed generically to Guidance Counselor, Wakefield High School; the return address said National Testing Service. It was a press release identifying two of Wakefield's finest as National Merit finalists, some Allison Kimble as well as one presently detained pothead.

"Those results could be your ticket into an Ivy League school, but the C's you're making in the classes you still bother to show up for around here aren't helping your case any," DeMouy said.

"Four years without any activities might not have them scrambling for their acceptance forms either," I suggested, though I was busy picturing myself with a sweater tied around my neck, sailing with Kennedys, desecrating human remains in some arcane Skull and Bones initiation rite.

"What happened in Texas?"

"What do you mean?" I stalled, startled by the new direction of his questioning.

"When this came in I was so sure they had the wrong Steve York that I did some checking into your records. According to your transcripts, you had a 4.0 through your first five semesters of high school. Near-perfect attendance. Then, the last semester of your junior year, it just falls apart. You even failed English III. Do you mind telling me how someone who makes a 760 verbal on his SAT fails English?"

"I couldn't make it all the way through *The Outsiders* again," I said. Suddenly I wasn't very comfortable in DeMouy's office.

DeMouy continued digging through my folder. "Your father is Alan York the astronaut."

"Is that a question?"

"Was he the third or fourth man to walk on the moon?" he said. "*That* is a question."

"I'll have to go home and check the trophy case. Though if you hear him tell the story, you'd swear he was first. This third or fourth thing may come as a big disappointment to him."

"You sound like you resent him."

"I don't *anything* him."

"Do you still think of Texas as home?" DeMouy asked.

"No."

I had moved to San Diego from Houston at the beginning of the summer. The astronaut had fought desperately for custody of me at the divorce hearing four years before. Sarah, my younger sister, was free to move with Mom to California, but the old man thought my future too important to trust to any non-hero. I was his heir. As such, I would be disciplined. I would study hard, excel in sports, choose my friends carefully, choose my college even more carefully. In short, bring glory to the York name.

I relocated to California after taking the last final exam of my junior year. I didn't go home or ask permission. I walked out of class, got in my El Camino, and drove twenty-seven hours nonstop until I reached the Pacific Ocean. The astronaut didn't even put up much of a fight when Mom called and told him I planned on staying. I imagine he had already seen his best laid plans turn to shit. My move allowed him the consolation of getting to share the blame.

"Where is home?"

I couldn't help it. I saw Dub's bedroom: the floor covered with jeans, T-shirts, and bras; the corkboard south wall supporting hundreds of tacked-on photographs, poems, and matchbooks from every club and roadside attraction Dub visited; her milk-crate-and-plywood desk supporting her prized PC; and most importantly, the door leading to her backyard. Always accessible, day or night— home.

"Wherever I lay my hat," I answered.

DeMouy glanced up from my file, but he kept his composure. I was certain the teen-hating, self-important, petty bureaucrat trapped inside the bodies of all educational administrators would soon appear. He scribbled something on a yellow legal pad.

"Do you realize you will be one English credit short at the end of the semester?" DeMouy asked.

"Yeah," I said casually, though I had been dreading that particular hurdle since transferring.

"Maybe we could work something out that would allow you to graduate on time," DeMouy said.

"Such as . . . ?"

I assumed he would want me to sign some sort of contract, something on official-looking stationery promising I wouldn't show up to school stoned. I'd sign it. I'd sign a contract promising not to breathe until graduation if it meant getting out of summer school.

"I want you to write a paper."

"How long does it have to be?"

"One hundred pages—"

"Excuse me?"

"That's one hundred *typewritten* pages. You do have a choice. Summer school would probably be easier."

"You don't want a paper; you want a novel."

"You get to choose the topic," DeMouy continued. "It can be fiction or nonfiction, an action adventure, a tale of teen angst and neglected cries for help. Though I would suggest you choose a topic you know something about."

"Who's going to grade this? If it's Mrs. Croslin, it can be a grocery list as long as I punctuate it correctly."

"You'll turn pages in to me, five to ten at a time," DeMouy said.

"Are you sure you're qualified? I mean, did all those years spent probing the teen mind leave any room for a true appreciation of literature?"

"I can manage. My first six years out of college I taught English. Now, I've never worked with a prodigy before, so you'll excuse me if I occasionally fail to grasp some of your especially esoteric passages."

Mrs. Martin, the school's human pumpkin of an attendance secretary, marched in without knocking. I could hear her panty hose–encased thighs rub together as she moved past me to hand a note to DeMouy. Through the open door I could see Sarah. Now if the principal were at all fearful of me, the bad seed, he should have been doubly so of Sarah. Ranked number one in her class and the first junior to be elected student council president, my sister wasn't satisfied with the ritual duties and perks her office bestowed upon her. Under her leadership, the student council no longer hung spirit posters or sold M&M's to pay for homecoming decorations. Earlier in the year she organized a walkout to call attention to the asbestos-laden dust being stirred up by the contractors who were charged with removing the offending tiles. Sixty percent of the student body didn't return after lunch. CNN even did a forty-five-second piece on it that included a fifteen-second soundbite from Sarah. That particular episode resulted in a call from the astronaut warning her that prestigious colleges didn't accept radicals. I think he was embarrassed because they identified her as his daughter.

Sarah spotted me in DeMouy's office and rolled her eyes. She rubbed one extended index finger across the other. Everything the astronaut wanted in his son had been inherited by his daughter, but the old man was too dumb to notice it. If another York were destined to walk on the moon, it was Sarah, not me.

"You'll be the only one who'll read it?" I asked DeMouy. My quick return to the subject at hand, I realized, was a potentially ruinous deviation from thrust-and-parry protocol involved in negotiations with adults.

"Promise," he assured.

"I'll think about it," I said coolly, picking myself up out of the chair and heading for the door.

"Steve."

"Uh-huh?"

"Don't think about it for too long. It's a limited time offer."

●●●

No one was around when I arrived home after school. This was the norm. Sis was out harassing school board members . . . something about vegetarian lunches in the cafeteria. Mother could have been anywhere in the hemisphere. Her marriage three years ago to a pilot for Delta had been a nonstop honeymoon. The fact that she married a commercial pilot impressed me as Mom's ultimate slap in the astronaut's face. I mean, talk about a giant leap down the scale of aeronautic nobility just to make a point. But month after month of weekend trips to Aspen or Acapulco had convinced Sarah and me there was more to her choosing this new husband, this "Chuck," than simply the revenge factor. I was lucky. I had only been constant witness to the past five months of the union. Sarah said during the first year she couldn't go anywhere with them—let alone have friends over—for fear the two would play tongue hockey in front of everyone.

I have always been, with the exception of students who failed a grade, the oldest in my class by at least a month. That may help explain, in part, why I'm so anxious to get out of high school. I'm nearly two years older than Sarah, though she's only one grade behind me. See, the astronaut thought I needed to be held back so that I would be more competitive in sports. Had I any interest in sports, I might be grateful; but as it stands, it will take me an extra year to get on with my life. Besides, I've hardly "filled out," as adults say of teen girls who get their breasts and boys whose arms, legs, and torso gain definition and sprout hair. Au contraire . . . *sleek, lean, rangy* all describe *this* physique, that is if you're kind. *Skinny, bony, scrawny, gawky* will work if you're not. Other than my pronounced lack of heft, I'm pretty nondescript: five-eleven, longish wavy brown hair, acne declining, wispy traces of headbanger mustache long since shaved off.

I'm "gifted." I know this because I was tested in junior high. Twelve of us so designated were isolated in separate classes, taught Latin phrases, allowed to use expensive telescopes, taken on field trips to ballets, and labeled complete geeks by our classmates. I'm sure the mental picture I'm creating is quite flattering: "Property of the Borg" T-shirt, overstuffed book bag. Am I close? I admit I've never been the dream date of anyone's homeroom, but it's not like I was the leading object of ridicule.

My ears are pierced, both of them. This in itself can be offered as explanation for the astronaut's failure to put up a fight when I moved west. The first earring was a bit trendy, I admit, but in constantly looking for ways to exist outside the mainstream, I was quick to take Dub up on her offer to complete the set, which she did one night with a leather stitching needle, two ice cubes, a potato, and bottle of hydrogen peroxide. There are those males who merely fill ear holes with tiny stones hardly big enough to offend a marine. Not me. Most days I wear big hoops. When I combine the look with a doo rag, I'm a regular pirate.

I grabbed a sleeve of Lorna Doones from the pantry and made my way upstairs to my room. Switching on the Macintosh I had received for my thirteenth birthday in lieu of the CD player I had requested, I sat down at my desk. Ninety minutes later I was staring at the fireworks screen saver that kicks in after five minutes of inactivity.

My one explosion of insanely brilliant creativity came in the form of a title for a story about a young bohemian relishing his first taste of life on the highway.

ROADS SCHOLAR
A novel by Steve York

After that, little came to me. I tried to imagine my first night driving off into nowhere. Who would I meet? What would they look like? More important, what rudely formed yet priceless gems of wisdom would pass from these people of the earth to the wing-footed young traveler? I struggled with several opening sentences. I immediately deleted, with one exception, each attempt. Though it pains me to do this, I'll offer one passage describing the "feel of the highway" that I saved for the comic-first-efforts preface to the posthumously issued *Collected Works of Steve York.*

He had been down roads to nowhere and alleys of sin. He had taken the high road and seen the light at the end of the tunnel, but only one stretch of pavement beckoned without respite—the one leading away from home.

Another thirty minutes passed.

Needing inspiration, I opened the dictionary, determined to begin my story with whatever word my finger landed on. I flipped to the middle and stabbed a page.

Oviparous: adj. Producing eggs that hatch outside the body.

Definitely time to give up. Reaching behind my Mac to switch it off, I remembered what DeMouy said before I left his office: Write about what I know. I've been told that a hundred times before. Sky said I needed to tattoo it to my right hand, so I would remember it every time I picked up a pen. "Science fiction," he would say, "is the only genre open to you imaginationalists"—a term he used to define the school of writing he said I was pioneering. If anyone knew I wouldn't have the stomach to write about spacemen, it was Sky.

Luke "Sky" Waters was the teacher of the creative writing elective I took the year before in Houston. In a way, Sky was more responsible than the astronaut for my relocation to California. He was Dub's teacher, too.

Sky had also maintained that all "true" writers had had their hearts broken. According to Sky's definition, I could become a writer now. My heart had been run through frappe, puree, and liquefy on a love blender. Dub had seen to that. Maybe I did have a topic capable of delivering me from summer school. I hoped DeMouy would appreciate what I was about to do. In order to bypass summer school, I was set to open wounds that had never really healed.

I began to type.

Houston, Freshman Year

When Mom and the astronaut called Sarah and me into our Cocoa Beach, Florida, (See *I Dream of Jeannie*) dining room to tell us they were getting a divorce, I admit I was shocked. I suppose I should have seen it coming, but the warning signs had been such a part of the status quo. I don't remember them ever being affectionate. Fights were a rarity, though had Mom gotten her way, I'm sure there would have been more. Peace prevailed outwardly because the astronaut was concerned about public appearances and would concede anything to avoid a confrontation in front of strangers. From my bedroom, I once eavesdropped on a battle royale. By pressing my ear to the air duct, I could hear them arguing about my future in Little League baseball. Mom fought hard to get me out of a third season of humiliation. The astronaut thought the experience would teach me important lessons about "stick-to-itiveness," teamwork, and self-confidence.

"Alan," she yelled at him, "you can't turn him into you."

But his mind was made up, and the two hadn't exactly set up their marriage as a democracy. I spent my third and final year of Little League alternating between right field (the least skill-intensive position and frequent spaz-repository) and the bench. Hearing Bobby Patton, our shortstop and cleanup hitter, beg the coach to bench me in an important game taught me volumes about self-confidence and teamwork.

Sarah, twelve at the time of the divorce conference, patted her father on the back (Mom actually did all the speaking. Alan was there to simulate a united front), and told him everything would work out for the best. I don't understand why her empathy was wasted on that barely animate statue.

The astronaut and I moved to Houston a few weeks after the divorce was final, but only forty-eight hours before my first day of high school. Houston was home base of NASA, and I had lived there before, back when he was still reveling in the celebrity he scored for doing the slow-motion moon hop, but I was too young to remember much about it. Besides, learning about Houston proper would have done little to prepare me for life in the tony suburb of Clear Lake, where we actually settled.

Most of the children of NASA lived in the area. The only black kid at Grace High was the son of one of the space shuttle pilots. Ours was a world of sports cars, designer clothes, fifteen-acre malls, million-dollar homes, cruising Westheimer on weekends, Galveston beach homes, and private tennis coaches.

●●●

My freshman year came and went, as freshman years tend to do, like a half-assed nightmare whose chief horror was endless, brain-rotting boredom rather than the expected *Blackboard Jungle* scenes in which brutal, leather-jacketed seniors would smash me against my locker and terrorize me:

> "Hey, Rocco, I smell somethin' bad. Waddya think it is?"

"I dunno, Paulie, dead fish maybe?"
"Nah, dis fish ain't dead—but he's gonna be!"

Nope. Nothing that exciting. I almost wish there had been.

Grace High School, "Home of the Buccaneers," dwarfed the junior high I'd attended the year before in Cocoa Beach. The school, only eight years old, still shined: no graffiti, no evidence of wear and tear. Freshmen were herded to the large gym to pick up schedules. Inside, booths had been constructed by every group conceivable, from the mundane (student council, glee club, future teachers) to the exotic (fantasy war gamers, Russian club, falconry club). There must have been fifty organizations there competing for freshman patronage.

The biggest relief upon receiving my schedule was knowing I would no longer be skimmed into special "think tank" classes. Nope, there it was in carbon—regular English, algebra, biology, etc. I'd be just one of the white, upper-middle class, spoiled, straight-toothed, Mazda Miata–driving wannabes. I'd fit right in.

As I made my way back through the throng (I had to begin searching for the English complex) I spotted perhaps the strangest of group structures—plywood supported by clumsily nailed two-by-fours arcing upward in nearly a 90-degree angle resembling an elongated U. At a table in front of this calamity of carpentry sat a refugee from a 1970s southern rock band—long straight blond hair, bangs hanging in front of his eyes, blue jean jacket, plain white T-shirt (not the designer Gap variety—the actual three-to-a-pack classic). He was, I noted with some surprise, reading. His book was called *Zen and the Art of Motorcycle Maintenance*. *Zen and the Art of Woodworking* would have been a wiser selection, I thought.

There was no prominently displayed sign demanding that we freshmen, like lemmings, line up to join whatever group this was.

"Is this where I sign up for wood shop?" I asked.

"Skate or Die," the Gregg Allman clone said.

"Right," I said, as if his response made perfect sense to me. "So what is this thing, anyway?"

Once questioned about the purpose of his structure, "Gregg" felt obliged to demonstrate. He kicked a skateboard out from under the table and began doing things on that ramp—flipping the board, spinning on his hand—I had only seen executed in rock videos. Soon I found myself at the epicenter of a hemisphere of gaping fourteen-year-olds. They were all new recruits for Skate or Die (which was, I learned, a club—Grace's purveyors of skateboard and diehard thrash-punk culture). Gregg, actually a fellow named Doug Chappell, had signed them up to replace alumni who had received their driver's licenses over the summer.

Although I never officially joined Skate or Die, on a social level I might as well have. Doug, the president and founder, became the nearest thing I had to a best friend, at least until I met Dub. Doug had formed Skate or Die because only recognized clubs got their pictures in the yearbook, and the school constitution required every officially recognized club to include fifteen members. He wouldn't have given a rat's ass about this had it not been for his annual five-hundred-dollar bet with his old man that Doug wouldn't get his picture in the book. Like the astronaut, Doug's parents fretted over their son's lack of popularity as well as his reluctance to participate in a high school social life they undoubtedly equated with malt shops and drive-ins. They had been, of course, joiners when they were his age. And though Doug won the yearbook bet, I'd be willing to make my own wager at the level of delight his parents took in his choice of peers. The Skate or Die club picture, which I'm certain the yearbook staff intentionally placed on the back side of a pizza coupon, featured sixteen scabby-kneed, male, potential "other cuts" models. I never set foot on a board, but I would follow them on a bike and hang out by the drainage ditch as they practiced maneuvers up and down its sides.

I didn't pose for the group picture or sign up on the roll that Doug had to turn in to the office. For almost exactly the same reasons Doug needed to be in the yearbook, I wanted to be excluded. I had a goal in mind—no activities would appear by my name in the yearbook.

My freshman year was rounded out by the landing of my first job—concessionaire extraordinaire at the Clear Lake Cineplex. There were so many things I loved about my job; where to start? Let's see, the red-and-white vertically striped shirt, the white paper Beetle Bailey cap, the button saying Steve at your service, or possibly the opportunity to pour rancid, fluorescent-hued nacho cheese for classmates who pretended not to know me.

•••

The most telling thing I can think of to say about the man who sired me is this: He walked three miles to school, uphill, both ways. With other adults, this would be hyperbole, but in the astronaut's case, it's true. He would walk to school at the highest point of Yakima, Washington (his birthplace, verifiable by the weathered Birthplace of Alan York legend on the "Now Entering" sign), then he would take a school bus down into the valley where he would pick grapes with the migrant workers before walking another three miles back home, uphill.

He might have stayed in Yakima his entire life if not for the first in a series of classic Alan York adventures. In a rare social excursion, he and a couple of friends went tubing down the Yakima River, which runs for thirty miles along the bottom of Kittitas Canyon. The river is notoriously dangerous, and given the number of drunken college students from nearby Central Washington University who float it, it's a wonder more don't drown than the annual average of two or three. To the point: Young Alan, in a feat that would today be re-created as an episode of *Rescue 911,* pulled some wasted college freshman out of the water and saved her life by administering CPR. Her uncle was an aide to the Republican senator from Washington who recommended the young do-gooder for the Air Force Academy. As if it could get any cheesier, the woman he saved was my mother. They dated most of my father's senior year in high school, married in the summer, and moved to Colorado in the fall of 1959.

Alan had had no time for sports and school hadn't challenged him. That changed at the academy. His scholarship gave him his first modest ration of free time, and rather than spend it with his new bride, he went out for the football team. Never mind that he'd played only sandlot ball, he had tenacity and spunk. He played quarterback or cornerback. One of those.

If you compare pictures of the astronaut from his last year of high school with ones from his first couple of years at the academy, it's as if he went through a second puberty that corrected all the shortcomings left by the first. He was as skinny as me in high school. Wiry, though. Hauling around grape crates had given him biceps. Other than girth, the change can be seen in his eyes. Though his expression doesn't change much over a fifty-five-year series of pictures (I defy you to find one where he's smiling), the images from his Yakima days suggest resignation, as if he's accepted a life of manual labor and debt. But over the next couple of years, he acquires two items indispensable for heroes: a glint and a chin. I can't explain where he got either, but he breezed up the ladder of military rank as a result. All this success landed him—now a captain—in Vietnam where he flew more than sixty bombing missions. He performed this task well enough to be decorated several times. Apparently his bombs killed more people than anyone else's bombs. Don't even get him started on Vietnam. He's of the we'd-have-won-if-they'd-only-let-us school of thought. He returned, became a test pilot, and then was asked to join the space program. The rest, as they say, is history, though in this particular case, it is literally so. If you want to read more, visit your local library. They'll be glad to help you.

San Diego, Senior Year

DeMouy's office was empty when I arrived Monday morning. He caught me, a few minutes later, on tiptoes peeking over the top shelves of his fern-covered file cabinet trying to discover from whence today's sounds of the jungle were emanating.

"Aren't you supposed to be somewhere, Steve?" he said.

"Anatomy. But I've got something for you." I held up the fern I had bought on the way to school once I knew I was going to be late. "This one raised his leafy arm and asked me to bring him to fern heaven."

"Bribery, the last recourse of the desperate," DeMouy said, taking the plant from me. The counselor found a spot on a bookshelf behind his desk for the latest addition to his floricultural collection.

"You offend me, sir; this is just my way of saying thanks. This technique you call literotherapy—it's the only thing keeping me off the hard stuff." Somewhere a macaw screamed. "So, tell me, which parts have you liked best?"

I wanted to know if he was really reading it or if he was another one of those grade-by-weighters.

"There have been so many good parts, where can I begin?" he answered. I viewed this as evasion.

"Did you like the part about me wanting to join the circus?" I asked.

"Yeah, that would have to be my favorite part," DeMouy said.

I smirked.

"Relax, Mr. York. I read it." He opened a drawer and tossed me the five-page printout. I could see comments written in green ink throughout the text. Green ink: The counselor knows his ed psych. We students subconsciously view red ink as aggressive and critical. Green ink comments merely represent advice from a kindly friend. Yoda would write in green ink.

I was gratified to learn DeMouy had a playful side and pleased I had overcome my initial qualms about planting a ganja seed in his fern. He wouldn't, however, write me a note excusing my tardiness to class.

San Diego, Summer Before Sophomore Year

In what would become an annual event, Sarah and I traded locales for the summer. Most of my time in San Diego I spent as my alter ego, Yard Boy. I mowed lawns, pruned trees, and weeded flower beds for the rental properties that Mom's real estate office managed. While it was grueling work, it did pay significantly better than peddling Junior Mints. I needed the money, as it was the only way I was going to get a car of my own. I had rejected the astronaut's less-than-attractive alternative method.

His offer: I play football; he buys me car. Now, to

hear him tell it, the greatest moments of his life were not spent bouncing around the lunar landscape; rather they were those brief instances in which he heard air rushing out of lungs as he separated Army pukes from pigskins. Football, he told me, required time and effort. It was almost impossible for a young man to devote the amount of time required by the sport and still hold down a job. Therefore, if I were to go out for the football team, he would understand how I might not have time for a job, and he knew how we teens needed to have a few dollars in our pockets.

Incidentally, when the astronaut said he would buy me a car, he was talking serious automobiliage, here. I could have been parking right up there in Miata row. Of course, mangled corpses can't really enjoy the fuel-injected madness a hot little sports coupe offers. I hoped the old fella's desire to see me in cleats and pads simply meant he didn't know what football players are like in a large Texas high school: one eye in the center of the fore-head, hair on their backs, fangs.

By the end of June I had saved almost thirteen hundred dollars. After weeks of circling potential Yorkmobiles, I found one that I knew I had to make mine. The initial attraction may have been our similar ages. We were both sixteen, the 1975 El Camino and I. She had a metallic purple paint job, an eight-track deck, and shag carpeting. Like a Transformer, she was half car, half truck. I spent twelve hundred dollars on the car and another hundred dollars on eight tracks at a used music store on the beach called Play It Again Sam's.

At the end of the summer, Mom decided she would ride to Texas with me to visit a friend (also a former Bride of NASA) for a couple days and then fly back to San Diego with Sarah. Thanks to overexposure to films like *Duel, The Texas Chainsaw Massacre,* and *Easy Rider,* she had been appalled by the idea of her soon-to-be sophomore son driving solo across a region peopled by cult murderers, gunslinging crackers, and homicidal truck drivers. The drive should have given the former Mrs. York and me some "quality time," but she was engrossed in some Danielle Steel novel. Driving was so thrilling to me, especially in new terrain, that I didn't mind the silence.

What I did mind was the astronaut's absence when we pulled into Château Sparse. When we'd called from San Antonio, Sarah had said he was there, but when we arrived in Houston four hours later he had vanished. He had been married to the woman for over thirty years, but he couldn't even stick around to say hello to her.

Sarah made some feeble excuse for the old man. He really wanted to see Mom, she said, but he got called into work. Mom stayed at the Hyatt for the next couple days, but the astronaut wasn't able to fit her into his remarkably hectic schedule. I drove Mom and Sarah to the airport, so his avoidance of his ex-wife was complete.

Funny thing, the man was looking good; his skin was bronze—a hue I didn't believe we York males were capable of attaining. In a futile effort at making the house more of a home, Sarah had magneted to the fridge several photos she shot during father-daughter weekend boating trips. Before returning to California, she gave the astronaut and me framed enlargements of her two favorite prints. The one she gave her father was of a salamander. The poor reptile had the misfortune of choosing our boat as a spot to sun itself. Sarah had tried to catch it and ended up pulling its tail off. (The shot of the disembodied salamander tail was displayed appetizingly on the refrigerator.) The twenty-four- by thirty-six-inch print given to the astronaut features the panicked lizard pressing itself to the glass in desperate hopes of avoiding the madwoman with the camera. My print was of a swan, wings stretched back, breaking the placid green of the lake. It was the only thing I hung up in my room.

Three girls arrived at the house to see Sarah off. One of them I recognized from school, the others I guessed were older. I had been in California for three months and had barely spoken to anyone my age. Sarah et al. hugged, wept, exchanged addresses.

Houston, Summer Before Sophomore Year

The colonial home in which the astronaut and I coexisted had five bedrooms. Keep in mind, only the two of us lived there. We never actually finished unpacking either. We unpacked only as necessity dictated. In other words, toilet paper was out first and things like artwork, photographs, and knickknacks probably remain in their boxes to this day. Imagine a house with nothing on its walls save a small photograph above the astronaut's desk of himself with President Nixon. No plants, no wall hangings—in short, nothing even remotely nonutilitarian. As a result, the house looked only temporarily occupied for the entire three years I slept there.

Initially we had eaten together and made feeble attempts at conversation. I had yet to meet anyone and couldn't think of any place else to be, and he hadn't been assigned to a project that could justify his working late. We settled into a more comfortable routine soon enough. He would leave for work before I woke but would provide a list of chores by the kitchen sink, paper-clipped to a ten-dollar bill, which was to provide me both lunch and dinner

This was the routine we fell into again when I got back from California. He did make one comment that surprised me. He said my time in California had begun to make a man out of me. I guess he was referring to my now recognizably male, if not Herculean, physique that had developed in some modest form due to the paces my summer employment put me through. In the mirror I could see the faint outline of a chest. Returning to form, however, he made his displeasure known about my choice of vehicle. An "eyesore," he called the El Camino. He also fondled my pierced earlobe, grimaced, and said he thought he had made it clear before I left Texas that I was to no longer wear an earring. That hole, he said, would have closed up had his edict been obeyed. I never wore an earring in his presence.

I returned to my low-paying yet leisurely job at the Clear Lake Cineplex; my enthusiasm delivering vertical movement within the company. I became the newest projectionist. This meant two things: I earned an extra quarter an hour and I got to watch movies. I only saw them in ten- to fifteen-minute slices, but with most of Hollywood's offerings, this was enough for me to adequately deduce the remaining seventy minutes.

A few days after I returned, the astronaut's morning note included two Houston Astros tickets along with the ten-dollar bill. "Be ready to leave for the game by six," the note said. The astronaut and I had never gone to a game—save my Little League efforts—together. Baseball I could comprehend if not play with distinction. The only sport I truly detested was football, and that was as much for the adulation bestowed upon its athletes in Texas as for the sport itself. Watching a baseball game in the oddly hermetic Astrodome would be fun regardless of my company.

As I could have predicted, the astronaut's seats provided a close-up view of jockstrap cup realignment, tobacco juice drool, and celebrity hobnobbing. George Bush sat three rows in front of us. He even gave the astronaut a little wave. George Strait was one section over, directly behind home plate. Charlie Sheen, a good buddy of one of the Astros infielders, sat a row in front of the former president between two savory Victoria's Secret models. The astronaut and I didn't have much to say but alternated trips to the concession stand and both whooped when Craig Biggio broke a tie with a sixth inning home run. All in all it was the closest thing to bonding we had done since our last fishing trip when I was nine (there the silence didn't seem so awkward). The public service announcer helped me clear my head of the damp, pastel-hued haze of sentiment during the seventh inning stretch.

"Ladies and gentlemen, please give a warm round of applause to astronauts Daniel Gary, Frederick March, and Alan York, who are here with their sons tonight as guests of the Houston Astros. Gentlemen, please stand and be recognized."

In the row behind us I saw two father-son teams stand in unison. I felt the astronaut get up beside me, and I heard the polite applause of twenty thousand baseball fans, but I, for one, wasn't going to function as the ceremonial family member trotted out to appease the apple pie set. I had seen Mom do it for too many years. I remained seated and ignored the *"Steves"* issuing from behind the astronaut's clenched teeth. We didn't speak a word to each other on the ride home from the game.

San Diego, Senior Year

They showed my school mug shot on the morning video announcements today as one of Wakefield's two Merit finalists. I was *so* stoned when that picture was taken. I had a bandanna pulled low over my sleepy eyes, and, in a dead giveaway, I was out of focus. My fellow anatomy students roared when the announcement was read. A couple smokers gave me the thumbs-up sign. Mr. Reyes shook his head resignedly.

Reyes was happy to get rid of me when a reporter from the Wakefield *Picayune* asked permission to interview me later in the period. The reporter, a nervous freshman named Henry, was working on his first "real" assignment. Before landing this exclusive, he had been in charge of the student opinion polls and school calendar listings. He led me down Wakefield's dreary, dimly lit corridors to the library where the other finalist sat waiting for us.

I waited for the journalist to introduce us, but he sat down and began fumbling through his notes.

"I'm Steve York," I said to my co-finalist, who was cuter than the picture they showed of her on TV.

"I know. I saw you on *Wake Up, Wakefield*." That was the name of the morning announcement/news show, but I'd never heard anyone refer to it so formally. "I'm Allison Kimble."

"Oh . . . I missed it this morning."

Henry began questioning us in a manner common, I'm sure, to staff writers for illustrious periodicals like *Teen Beat* and *16*. He wanted to know such vital data as favorite places to study and noteworthy hobbies. The brain-locked frosh asked no follow-up questions. Rather, he plowed heedlessly through his scripted line of inquiry, paying little if any attention to our responses.

"Steve, were there any major turning points in your life?"

"Let's see, Henry. I guess when I knocked over that liquor store in seventh grade. . . ."

"And your favorite subject?"

"Wood shop."

The legitimate biographical information he garnered in our twenty-minute interview would have fit nicely onto the back of a National Merit finalist trading card. Allison said her favorite author was J. D. Salinger. (How teenaged of her.) I said mine was Gore Vidal. (How deviant of me.) Allison said her hero was her father. I said my hero was also, coincidentally, Allison's father. Allison rolled her eyes.

When Henry asked Allison what she wanted to be when she grew up, my intellectual rival lost her patience with the cub reporter. She snatched Henry's notebook, scanned the list of remaining questions, then swiveled toward me to complete the interview herself. I adopted a countenance that suggested a renewed interest in the proceedings.

Clearing her throat, she managed to replicate Henry's grave tone. "If you could be any barnyard animal, what barnyard animal would you be?"

"Rooster," I answered, resisting my urge to use a synonym.

"Uh-huh . . . and the sum of two and two is?" She held up two fingers on each hand to help me out.

"Four?" I replied, letting my voice register a shred of hope.

Henry clued in. "Hey, I've gotta get this stuff. Even if you think it's stupid." He looked as if he might sob. Allison and I glanced at each other. She bit her lower lip and lowered her head like a frequently backhanded mutt. I likewise tried to appear repentant.

"Go ahead, Henry. We're sorry," Allison offered.

Henry composed himself, reshuffled his notes, and, in his dinky freshman falsetto, continued. "Where do you plan on going to college?"

Allison: "Stanford, Northwestern, maybe Princeton."

Steve: "San Diego Community College."

Allison's trading card was filling up much quicker than mine. She had been on the Academic Decathlon team, was an officer for the Latin Club, and a founder of the Wakefield SADD chapter.

"And what about you, Steve?" Henry asked, number-two pencil poised.

"I just transferred here this year."

"What did you belong to at your old school?"

"GOD," I said.

Houston, Summer Before Sophomore Year

Doug and I had gotten our driver's licenses within a week of each other. Though he was a grade ahead of me, I was four days older. Upon returning to town I called to find out what he had in store for Skate or Die. First of all, I asked, did we really want to be seen with freshmen?

"I don't really want to be seen with sophomores," was Doug's sardonic reply.

The thought of sneaking cases of Busch down into the suburban waterway system to share in malodorous, centipede-infested darkness with fourteen cast alternates from *River's Edge* inspired us to seek a new direction. But figuring out an alternative proved difficult.

"Remind me again why the League of Women Voters won't grant us a chapter," Doug said. He was still pissed that his original idea, though brilliant in concept, wasn't going to reach fruition.

"I called their office. They said the founders of any chapter had to be registered voters, and, as surprising as this may sound, women."

Doug had seen the LWV as a surefire way to meet

girls, and not just girls of our ilk—no, genuine letter-jacket-wearing, pep-rally-attending, rosy-cheeked "gals." What mangy, head-banging Doug and I would do with these gals once we met them was a question we left unanswered. We had already rejected the Pete Best Fan Club ("too retro") and the Sons of the Cold War ("too political").

Losing faith in our ability to come up with anything inspired, Doug decided to raid his parents' stock of Red Stripe, a Jamaican beer they had developed a taste for on one of their frequent escapes from Doug and his older brother, Stan, Jr. As we walked into the house I caught the familiar lime-green neon glow of Doug's skateboard sticking out of a slab of seashell-laced concrete.

"What's this?" I said, pointing to what used to be my friend's sole means of transportation.

"Art," he said.

"Sort of a *Tomb of the Unknown Skater*?"

"More like *Headstone of the Unknown Skater*," Doug said, pausing to take a look at the juxtaposition. "It's nothing, really. I broke my board a couple weeks ago when I was working on the Hawthorne pool. (Doug worked for his parents at Clear Lake Pools and Spas.) We were pouring stepping-stones for a walkway, and I just stuck half the board into the concrete before it set. Voilà. *C'est fantastique.*" Doug had taken French while I was in typing.

"You're a real dadaist," I said.

"*Excusez-moi?*"

"A dadaist," I repeated. "We studied them in my egghead classes in Florida. They were painters, writers, sculptors in the twenties who believed in art without coherent meaning. Nothing they did had to be justified. The more abstract, the weirder something was, the better."

"So if you, as the art critic, were to say my master-piece here represented the death of a subculture or a man putting away childish things, I, as the artist, would say . . ."

"Sod off, wanker. It's a skateboard in concrete," I concluded for him in my best Sid Vicious cockney snarl.

"I love it! Art for the masses."

Houston, Sophomore Year

Doug and I watched with equal measures of wistfulness and bemusement as the crowd of freshmen gathered in front of the skateboard ramp we had willed to Junior Cassidy. We couldn't see much from our spot across the gym—only Junior's head as he spun at the top of each run—but we heard the requisite "*oohs*" from Grace High's newest fodder.

"We might be making a mistake," I said to Doug. We were wearing our homemade T-shirts freshly emblazoned with our club slogan, GO WITH GOD. Like I'M WITH STUPID shirts, our uniforms included arrows. My arrow pointed toward Doug, assuming I could keep him on my left; Doug's pointed down toward . . . well, hell is where he said, though I think most of us would agree his crotch was the first whistle-stop on that journey.

GOD was the name Doug coined for our new club, the Grace Order of Dadaists. No one had yet ventured over to our table. Several frightened ninth graders had stood at a safe distance and pointed at the artwork Doug and I displayed. The first was the original skateboard tombstone. The second, our pièce de résistance, was what I believed was scaring everyone. On a television monitor we ran a video Doug and I had produced. By editing together half-second clips of happy teenagers garnered from fast food, soda, and jeans commercials then splicing in machete, arrow, and axe mutilation scenes from Stan's collection of teen slasher films and scoring it with Louis Armstrong's "What a Wonderful World," we had created a grotesque and mystifying barrage of images. I was glad we, as dadaists, were not obliged to explain it.

When freshman orientation ended we had yet to hand out any of our brochures, let alone sign up one member. Skate or Die, on the other hand, had swelled its membership to twenty-plus. Junior wouldn't be back the next day for the registration of the rest of the student body. GOD would be.

During the first couple hours of nonfreshmen orientation, events proceeded not unlike the day before. We were fortunate the larger crowds forced more students nearer our booth; it wasn't long before plucky individualists hovered long enough to pick up our brochures. Doug and I had had our first philosophical argument concerning GOD four days earlier when he suggested I produce a brochure on my Mac. I argued that true dadaists would never produce sensical prose in hopes of increasing their numbers. Their art, I insisted, would serve as their calling card. He maintained, and rightly so I discovered later, that the original dadaists, our spiritual forefathers, had written at great length about their contribution to the art world. Because we were dealing with his five-hundred-dollar bet and he had already checked out and read *Dada: In Theory, in Practice,* I relented.

On the opening fold of the brochure I placed a black-and-white photo of the intellectual founder of dadaism, Tristan Tzara, above the headline, GOD ISN'T FOR EVERYONE. Inside, Doug drew his own crude rendition of Marcel Duchamp's bicycle wheel installations above lists of relatively famous dadaist painters, sculptors, authors, and performance artists. Doug and I collaborated on the inside copy, which read:

DADAISM IS NOT DEAD!

- DID YOUR SECOND-GRADE TEACHER SCOLD YOU FOR COLORING AN APPLE PURPLE AND THE SKY RED, THUS DESTROYING YOUR ARTISTIC URGES? IF SO, GO WITH GOD.
- DO PAINTINGS OF MEDIEVAL NOBLEMEN OR DREAMY RENAISSANCE-ERA PANORAMAS OF EUROPEAN COUNTRYSIDES ALL BEGIN TO LOOK THE SAME TO YOU? IF SO, GO WITH GOD.
- DO *PREDICTABLE, MUNDANE, ORDINARY, COMMON,* AND *ROUTINE* SOUND LIKE BAD WORDS TO YOU? IF SO, GO WITH GOD.

THE QUESTION ALL OF US SHOULD BE ASKING OURSELVES IS NOT WHY, BUT RATHER, WHY NOT?

I left my post for a few minutes to pick up my sophomore schedule. Upon returning, I was surprised to see a fair-sized crowd of potential dadaists clustered around our booth. Doug was in the process of explaining dadaist doctrine to three girls.

"What's the point?" the shortest of the three said. I was sure I recognized her from somewhere, but I couldn't place her.

"Exactly!" Doug answered. The conversation sounded remarkably like Abbott and Costello's "Who's on First?" skit.

"So, what you're saying is this video, this skateboard thing, there's no meaning behind them?" She was trying to understand. "Are they even supposed to evoke a certain reaction?"

"Not a *certain* reaction," Doug said, "just *a* reaction."

Then it happened. Doug was set upon by the president of the Fellowship of Christian Athletes. With fists clenched around the GOD brochure, he began shouting before he reached our booth.

"Did you write this? Did you write this?" he ranted, slapping the brochure across his left hand. "God is for everyone. Everyone!"

I was suddenly happy Doug was the de facto leader of this group and I was merely an unofficial member. Predictably, Doug made the most of the spotlight.

"You're wrong, brother." My comrade matched his accuser's volume as he quoted an early draft of our brochure. " 'GOD is not for fascists, clones, wannabes, television junkies, spirit heads, or for that matter, zealots.' "

"Atheist," the FCA president croaked.

"No," Doug said, "dadaist."

Most of the crowd didn't know what to make of the exchange, but the FCA faculty adviser confiscated our brochures and made Doug and me take off our shirts and wear them inside out.

"I guess that's what you mean by *a* reaction," said the short girl who had been questioning Doug. I finally remembered where I had seen her. She was one of the girls who'd said good-bye to my sister when she left Texas.

She signed her name, Wanda Varner, on our club membership roll; her two friends signed up after her. They beat the rush. Doug's eloquence convinced fourteen of what I assumed to be the school's disenfranchised to join up. Fourteen, however, was the number I dreaded most. We needed fifteen members, and the onus was on me to provide the last signature. As we walked to the office to apply for our charter, I told Doug I would relent and sign. "Don't worry," he said. "It's taken care of." He took out the list and signed "Tom Pittman" at the bottom.

"Who's that?" I asked.

"The president of the FCA," he answered.

• • •

Wanda Varner sat in front of me in geometry. Of course, everyone sat in front of me in geometry. My punctuality on the first day of classes was owed completely to my desire to sit in the back of the classroom. Luckily, my last name usually protected me from anal-retentive teachers who insisted on alphabetical-order seating charts. I liked it when it took a teacher nearly a semester to learn my name. Not speaking, not volunteering answers, not turning in especially brilliant homework—I should market my anonymity strategy. I remember my mother coming home angry from a mandatory, early-morning, parent-teacher conference because my teacher couldn't, for the life of her, remember who I was despite the A I was making in her class.

Teachers all call me Steven. They do this because I don't correct them on the first day of school when all the Jonathans change to Jacks and the Roberts become Bobs. On the first day of geometry, Wanda became Dub. When she said it, Mrs. Lanigan flinched.

"Did you say 'Bud,' honey, as in 'Rosebud'?"

"No. I said 'Dub,' as in 'rub-a-dub-dub.' "

Most of the class turned to look at this strange girl. If she were pretty, she did her best to hide it. Her hair was black, but it was the jet black that indicated the original color was smothered in dye. She wore no makeup. She dressed in men's blue jeans a couple sizes too big and a Rice (Houston's Harvard of the South) sweatshirt—also oversized. At the risk of sounding redundant, her mouth, too, was uniquely large, but she had those puffy, Uma Thurman lips which, judging from recent *Sassy* cover models, was the current standard of beauty. What else? Green eyes, B cup, small feet, no jewelry, *Whole Earth* backpack—the kind favored by outdoorophiles or the studious, as its capacity is sufficient to store the complete *Encyclopedia Britannica*.

Seven days later she spoke to me.

"So, you're not really an asshole?"

I scanned my active snappy-comeback file but came up empty. I looked like a goob, standing in the doorway of Mrs. Lanigan's class, mouth open, saying nothing.

"Speak boy, speak," Dub beckoned. She even patted her thighs encouragingly. She was pleased with how our initial conversation was proceeding.

"Who said I was an asshole?" I managed.

"I just sort of deduced it," Dub answered. "We've seen plenty of each other. The first time I saw you, you looked like you wanted to kill somebody—you were taking Sarah to the airport. Then, you didn't say anything to me when I joined your club. And now you've sat behind me for a week, and you still don't say a word. I'm like, who does the boy think he is—Sting?"

"What made you decide now that I'm not so bad?" It occurred to me *she* hadn't spoken to *me* on any of these occasions, either.

Dub began walking to her next class, and I followed though it was the wrong direction. "I told Sarah in a letter what an egomaniac I assumed you were. She wrote back that you weren't all that bad. She said you just don't say much."

"Oh." (Good ol' Sis.) "Wait a minute. I've been meaning to ask. Why do you call yourself Dub if your name is Wanda?"

"With a name like Wanda, my only career options were running point for a roller derby team or waitressing at a truck stop."

"But why 'Dub'?" I said, realizing I was going to be late to world history.

"I started signing all my papers 'W. Varner.' People began calling me 'W.' It just got shortened to 'Dub,' " she said. "So, when are we going to have our first meeting?"

"Meeting of what?"

"GOD, dork," she said. I didn't know if I liked a stranger establishing pet names this early in a relationship. "We *are* planning on entering a float in the homecoming parade, aren't we? Every other club, except Skate or Die, is."

The bell rang, and I realized I was standing in Dub's amused English class. Dub, on first meeting, had already subjected me to public humiliation and a tardy slip. I should have recognized the omen. On the bright side, the bell prevented me from answering the question. I mean, could you see me working on a homecoming float?

◆ ◆ ◆

"She wants to do what?" Doug said between cheese Tater Tots. We had been hitting the Sonic Drive-in daily for lunch. We parked on the "nerd" side and made fun of the socials who sat in the sun on the "cool" side.

"She thinks we ought to enter a float in the homecoming parade," I answered.

"I tell you. The chick is wigging. I mean, imagine it: a big banner across a flatbed truck with you and me sitting on a couple bales of hay, smiling and shouting 'Beat the Mustangs!'" Doug was waving food around the El Camino. "Tell her to join the Buccaneer Babes if she wants to bake cupcakes for football players." Doug paused. "On the other hand, tell her we think her idea is keen or boss or rad—"

He could have gone on, but I interrupted. "You're the pope. You tell her."

"Better yet, we'll call a meeting. We'll explain true dadaist canon to the acolytes."

Calling a meeting—we hadn't done this before; it presented new challenges. With Skate or Die, the skaters just hung out in the same places they always had. Fundraising had involved emptying everyone's pockets of excess lunch money to pay for beer or spray paint. Neither of us had contemplated anything but the inception of GOD. Responsibility, we sensed, loomed.

"How do other clubs call meetings?" Doug asked in the dejected manner of a visionary asked to pay for his program.

"They make morning announcements. Generally, they shoot for cuteness, like 'The chess club will hold its monthly *board* meeting today at lunch' or 'The Grace Thespians will get their *act* together after school in the theater.' A witty, yet newsy, directive."

Though I remained a nonmember, Doug put me in charge of publicity. The following day I acquired an announcement form from an insanely pleasant receptionist. The real chore, though, was composing suitably dadaistic prose. The end product, approved by Doug, read: "Avalanche the ghost roper! Defy Mother Nature and her minions. Dadaists unite in secular purgatory, Pizza Hut, tomorrow night at 6."

The principal in charge of reading announcements required several attempts before completing the announcement. The only two words he enunciated clearly were *Pizza* and *Hut*.

Dub looked back at me as the announcement was completed. "So when did avalanche become a verb?" she asked.

Pizza Hut, with its uniform, vinyl, mansard-roofed architecture, might not have seemed the most felicitous setting for the birth of a society bent on the overthrow of convention. "All You Can Eat" was a powerful draw, however, and we were sans the faculty advisor who could secure us classroom space for a meeting on campus. I didn't really expect people to show. If Doug and I hadn't foreseen GOD being an active club, why would anyone else? So I was surprised to see our complete roster, with the expected exception of FCA prez, Tom Pittman, at the meeting. Nine girls, five guys—six if you included me—the times they were a-changing.

As this was the first assembly of GOD, few of the members knew one another. Chitchat reached the din we associate with spearfishing Eskimos or cloistered monks. Still, I felt antsy. I had this awful vision of Doug standing and clinking his glass with his spoon to get everyone's attention. If we weren't careful we had the potential to slip into mainstream high school participatory bullshit. We'd be following *Robert's Rules of Order* and exchanging friendship gifts with GOD squads from rival schools at halftimes of basketball games before we knew what hit us. But, I reminded myself, that's why we had called this meeting—to nip any thoughts of activism in the bud. The contradiction was easy to spot, though; we were having a meeting to let members know we wouldn't be meeting.

Without standing and without raising his voice, Doug began what I imagined would be the first and last meeting of the Grace Order of Dadaists.

"Welcome to Cabaret Voltaire," Doug said, confusing everyone. Cabaret Voltaire was the name of the club Tristan Tzara had contributed work to in Zurich in the twenties, a haven for fellow dadaist painters, poets, and performance artists. "My name is Doug Chappell and I'm an alcoholic." He got a laugh. The standard conventioneer icebreaking opening joke. Would he follow with the one about the traveling salesman? "I thought we needed to get together to talk about the goals we have for GOD." *Goals?* Doug scanned the table. "GOD, as you probably already know, is not for everyone. Like our artistic forefathers, we are concerned with the destruction of established mediums. In other words, our goals should include nonparticipation in anything established society—in our case, school—presents. Dances, canned food drives, campus cleanups"—Doug looked right at Dub—"parades—these are anathema to the true dadaist."

"I suppose dadaists wouldn't pose for yearbook photos either," Dub said.

Touché.

"I know about your bet with your parents. I have friends in Skate or Die. I respect the lengths you'll go to to win, I really do, but don't sermonize about the rules of dadaism when *your* motives are impure."

I was floored by the onslaught. Doug handled it gracefully.

"A yearbook photo is different from a parade. We're subverting the system by appearing in a book they want exclusively for homecoming queens and football stars. A float only serves as further glorification of the status quo." Doug shook his head in a most fatherly no as he spoke his last sentence. He mistakenly thought he was having the final say.

"Wrongo," Dub said. Dub sat at one end of the tables we had pushed together. Doug sat at the other. The rest of us were forced to rotate our heads in tennis spectator fashion in order to follow the action. "You are assuming our float would be like the floats of the student council and the Key Club and the German Club. That's where you're mistaken. We wouldn't put a giant buccaneer on the float. We wouldn't sit up there and grin like idiots. Our float would be a giant rolling sample of dadaistic art. We *would* be subverting the system. Think about it—a giant rolling carrot or maybe just a flatbed truck with nothing on it but a six-pack of generic cola."

"Or how about the word 'elbow' spelled out in carnations?" said one of the males of the group sitting next to me.

"Or maybe we could get a bunch of people lined up

on the float dressed and acting like they were watching a parade," offered one of Dub's friends. "That way the people watching the parade could see how ridiculous they look." I could tell we had a budding performance artist.

"That would be more surreal than dadaistic," Dub suggested to her friend. Dub turned her attention back to Doug. "Anyway, there are a million good ideas for the float, but my overall point here is this: We should participate in every cheesy event the school lobs up to us. But every time they do, we put our own spin on it. I don't want to be in a club just to get my picture in the yearbook; we should produce dadaistic art. We should open our own Cabaret Voltaire where we exhibit our art, and anyone else's for that matter. We should lead the cultural revolution at Grace."

Dub had accomplished with Doug what it had been infinitely easier to do to me: She left him speechless.

Doug and I discussed the ramifications of the meeting on the ride home from the Hut.

"That sure didn't go the way I planned it," Doug said.

"I must say I admire how you took control in there," I said. "Now, which committee did Dub put you on? Are you in charge of refreshments?"

Doug was missing the humor. "Maybe I should resign."

"Shut up! You are *such* a big wuss. What's bothering you the most here? That she was right? Or was it that she took charge?" Sometimes Doug's need to lead got the better of him.

For the twelfth time during the last hour, Doug took off his John Deere cap, removed the rubber band from his long blond ponytail, and shook his hair out, letting it fall in front of his face; pulled his hair tightly back into a ponytail, re-rubber-banded it; and weaved it above the adjustable straps of his cap.

"Either that or laziness. Do you want to spend your free time working on a float?" he said.

"With nine girls? Yeah, I do." It was an easy decision for me. "Look, you're an idea man. You haven't lost control of the club; you just need to rethink your goals a bit."

"That girl is something else, isn't she?" Doug said.

"Frightening."

San Diego, Senior Year

As my chemistry teacher lectured, I began casually changing the Styrofoam and Tinkertoy water molecule models on display along the back wall into kryptonite (the formula and structure were revealed in *Superman* #178). An office aide relieved the monotony by requesting my presence in the counselor's office.

If you knew what you were looking for in DeMouy's office, you could spot the eight-inch-high nonfern easily. I'll say this for marijuana: Given plenty of light, nutrient-primed soil, and consistent watering, it will shoot up like, well . . . a weed. DeMouy stood peering into the top drawer of his desk as I entered. His long sigh at seeing me indicated my visit was business, not pleasure.

"Sometimes, Steve," he began, "we sow seeds born of desperation and rage that, as older and wiser souls, we eventually regret."

So this is where this is heading, I thought.

"This idea is planted in our head—we can walk away without minding the crop, but unless that crop is harvested, the reaper will indeed be grim," DeMouy continued his allegorical lecture. He ended by looking me straight in the eye. "*Capisce*, Grasshopper?"

If I was reading his sermon correctly, I knew what I needed to do.

"Look! I think I see a troubled teenager considering self-destructive behavior," I said, gesturing toward the window.

DeMouy obliged me by turning around. I quickly stepped around his desk and pulled the ganja out by its roots.

"Grasshopper," DeMouy said, still facing the other direction.

"Yes, honorable master?" I said, stuffing the offending plant up my sleeve.

"Leave it in the wastebasket."

Houston, Sophomore Year

With the exception of its leader, GOD's members were exhibiting an esprit de corps I had never experienced firsthand. We spent two to three hours each Monday through Thursday in the porta-barn owned by the parents of the Whiteside brothers, Bill and Matt. Beverly Shoaf's parents bred horses, and she was able to talk them out of their flatbed trailer for the last two weeks of September through the mid-October homecoming game. I probably could have asked for the *Apollo 3* spacecraft had I told the astronaut I was working on a homecoming float. Instead I explained my late hours by saying I was filling in for a vacationing co-worker at the 'Plex.

Initially I assumed my fellow dadaists had joined the group for the same wiseass reasons Doug and I had founded it, but as I got to know my comrades, I learned their motivations were as varied as the members themselves. Possibly the sole thing we had in common was a need to be challenged. Let's face it, outwitting school officials doesn't require more than ten or twelve brain cells. To be the cleverest member of GOD, though, now that would be a big deal.

Because you can't tell your nihilist without your program . . .

Rhonda Smith: Dub friend number one. Rhonda consistently dressed two days behind Dub (i.e., Dub wears peasant dress Monday; Rhonda wears peasant dress Wednesday). Has resisted urge to dye her red hair black, however. Tardy but eventual participant in all activities Dub-borne.

Missy Carmical: Dub friend number two. Missy offered the Pizza Hut idea of peopling the float with faux parade spectators. If Rhonda represented Dub's superego, Missy was the id. Nothing was too radical for Missy: see-through dresses with black bras, experimental drug use. Rumored to have lost virginity as sophomore to member of Material Issue after show at Fitzgerald's.

Beverly Shoaf: Daughter of Unitarian ministers, she was inspired by Doug's showdown with Tom Pittman, who she had always considered an ass. Spoke little, but was right on the money when she did. Least *hip* member of group. She dressed in early dowdy.

Zipper: No one ever took the time to explain the difference between punk and new wave to Zipper. She worshipped both Richard Hell and Robert Smith. She wore only black and shot for a complexion just on the eggshell side of pale. Bandied about the word "conformist" like she was getting paid for each usage.

Virginia Cole: Like Zipper, Virginia joined GOD hoping it would serve as an "anticlub"—a club for social misfits and badge-flashing losers. Saw everything as "us versus them," the haves versus the have-nots. Of course, when your house borders the fifth fairway of the Clear Lake Country Club golf course, as hers did, feigning populism doesn't get you far.

Holly Cooper: One of three seniors in the group, Holly was the editor of the *Grace Gazette,* the school's newspaper. She was also in the running for valedictorian, but needed to beat out fellow GOD member and debate partner, Samantha Ellis.

Samantha Ellis: Though I never saw the two of them in action, I've heard they dismantled opponents in such ruthless fashion that they often broke into finals without having to win a match: rival debate teams saw Ellis/Cooper as their draw and simply scratched. Samantha, along with Dub, represented the active feminist segment of GOD. Male members learned quickly to call our female members "women" lest we be called "boy" in withering tones.

Lynnette Sirls: Mistook us for the art club, but gamely stuck with GOD through the first semester despite never quite grasping the notion of dadaistic expression. We lost her to the cute shortstop of the JV baseball team, but not before Lynnette completed, at the coaxing of Doug, a papier-mâché *Rabbit in Punchbowl* which we installed in the Cabaret Voltaire display case.

Veg: Ben Kempler (aka Veg) refused to eat meat strictly on moralistic grounds. Some said, though I never witnessed this, that he apologized to vegetables before downing them. Before his conversion, Veg had been a chicken-fried-steak-a-day man and had the spare tire that often accompanies such a diet. By the time I met him, he could have been sharing clothes with Ghandi. Veg split his free time between GOD and the Houston chapter of Greenpeace.

Bill Whiteside: Bill was the Renaissance man of GOD. He had disassembled his pickup's engine and put it back together, for fun. His forte was physics, but he hadn't limited his knowledge to the sciences. Bill played guitar, was an assistant editor of *Buried Treasure,* the Grace literary magazine, and had the lead in the school play.

Matt Whiteside: As a rule, my interest in nonmainstream sexuality runs no deeper than your standard state trooper's, but I always found it hard not to stare at Matt Whiteside, a Chippendale-without-portfolio who was quite possibly the best-looking guy in school. He wasn't, however, the Mr. Everything his brother was. He was smart, but in Doug's and my opinion, he wasted too much of his energy worrying about grades. By the end of the year Doug was calling him "Ivy," as in "Ivy-League bound." I think Matt liked the nickname, though I'm quite certain Doug hadn't meant it as a compliment.

Trey Collier: Our one athlete, Mike Collier was the designated gunner on the varsity basketball team. "Trey" stemmed from his marksmanship beyond the nineteen-foot, nine-inch, three-point arc. Trey hadn't joined GOD as any form of antiestablishment protest. Au contraire, the boy dated a Buccaneer Babe, listened to Bon Jovi, and drove a Camaro. Trey was, in a sense, the only "pure" member of GOD. He joined because he was fascinated with dadaistic art. No one needed to explain the work of Duchamp to him. Trey took art three periods a day if you include the period he was Mr. Harley's aide.

While he may have been disgruntled, Doug wasn't pouting. He put himself in charge of bureaucratic concerns—applying for a float permit, attending the drawing of parade order, picking up the list of rules, supplying the thirty-dollar registration fee. Fifty-dollar prizes would be awarded in three categories: grand champion, most spirited, and most original.

We had no doubt the float we were constructing would be the most original, but as members of GOD, we harbored little hope of winning the cash. What would the judges think of our entry? We discussed at length what direction we wanted to go with the float before critiquing the sketches offered by Dub (man-sized numerals arranged in the order of a phone number drawn at random from the Houston phone book), Samantha (a giant football player dressed in Grace's blue and gold; the hitch?—the linebacker was pushing a baby carriage), and Lynnette (the standard Grace Buccaneer broncobusting a Memorial Mustang—she was still unclear on the tenets of dadaism). We settled on Trey's sketch of a carpenter's claw hammer long enough to extend from the rear of the trailer and have its head positioned directly above the cab of the truck. The sketch evoked different reactions in all who observed it. Given its angle and red handle, I likened it to the hammer and sickle of the old Soviet Communist Party. Missy was struck by the "raw sexual energy," Zipper the violence, and Lynnette the notion Grace would hammer the Mustangs. Holly, with perception nearest the artist's intentions, liked the clean lines.

Bill converted the naysayers by offering to modify the concept a bit.

"You know," he said, holding the sketch in both hands, "with a lawn mower engine and a couple bicycle gears, I could make this hammer swing up and down like it's bashing in the cab of the truck."

As if any of us needed more reason to feel superior, the speed, efficiency, skill, artistic vision, and wit with which our float proceeded only served to cement our hubris. But our newfound loyalty to GOD didn't owe primarily to the quality of the project. I think what we experienced was one part Amish barn-raising enthusiasm and one part Chicano gang member group reliance. We went to lunch with fellow dadaists. We waved at each other in the halls. We sat next to each other in classes we shared.

As I abandoned my initial aloofness, Dub and I began an ongoing game in geometry. We took turns foretelling the futures of our classmates. These ran from standard hipster slagging, "She'll be the first woman to actually give birth to 2.2 children," to epics nearly always ending in slapstick death. Dub killed off an especially perky front rower with invading laser-toting Neptunians who regarded hand-raising as a hostile act. Normally, the trouble with becoming acquainted through the taunting ritual is that you're forced to temper your pithiness lest you A) reveal yourself as a stone-hearted asshole or B) accidentally offend your cohort. Dub would have none of that dewy-eyed compassion shit. She went for blood.

I no longer feared Dub (okay, not as much); she was a kindred spirit. Rhonda, however, intimidated the hell out of me. She was sending out signals I was not too green to interpret: I would catch her staring at me; she would stand in my very American-sized personal space when speaking to me; she kept finding reasons to touch me, whether it was to try on one of my earrings, rub my shoulder to get my attention, or once, to pull my wallet out of my back pocket to get money for extra paint. Before I could say anything, she pulled out a five and announced that I didn't believe in safe sex.

San Diego, Senior Year

The Wakefield *Picayune* came out today. Among other things, it said that, "York, an active member of a church group at his previous school in Texas, plans to attend a local community college. He sees a career in high school counseling in his future."

Houston, Sophomore Year

Friday and Saturday nights were normally sacrosanct. Doug had arranged our float work schedule so as to allow social lives, or in my case, enable me to supplement my meager, by Clear Lake standards, allowance. But with a week remaining before the parade, it was obvious we

needed the weekend to complete *Get Hammered*—
which had become the working title of our rolling tribute
to dadaism. I finagled the Saturday off.

The mechanics of the basher assembly had proven
more intricate than Bill had originally envisioned, but
eventually we had the chicken-wire-and-wooden-dowel
hammer frame smacking the roof of the cab every six seconds. The first of the weekend nights my comrades spent
papier-mâchéing the hammer; the second night we painted. We completed the job by midnight. Seven of us were
there to see the GOD float project reach fruition: the
Whitesides, Dub, Missy, Rhonda, Doug, and I. The rest we
lost to fatigue, weekend jobs, dates, and, in Holly's case,
the following morning's administration of the SATs. The
Dub Club came prepared for the grand finale. As Bill
brushed the final layer of silver paint across the hammer's
claw, Missy pulled three bottles of champagne out of
Dub's black hole of a backpack. Dub dug further into the
sack and emerged with plastic champagne glasses—the
kind in which the stem snaps into the bowl.

"El Presidénte"—Dub curtsied and handed the bottle to Doug—"would you do the honors?"

"Ah, but yes, fair maiden," said Doug as he relieved
Dub of the bubbly, purloined earlier from Missy's
parental liquor cabinet. Doug's cavalier demeanor was
quickly replaced by that of a sea dog. When the cork,
once shucked of its foil and wire binding, didn't give way
to nimble tugs, our leader stuffed the bottle top in his
mouth, growled, and pulled the offending cork out with
his teeth.

"How boorish," Missy observed.

"*Très gauche,*" added Dub.

Our glasses wouldn't give us the onomatopoeic sat-
isfaction of a *clink,* but toasts abounded nonetheless. We
christened *Get Hammered* in the name of Marcel

Duchamp, Stanley Hardware, Inc., and GOD almighty. We all sat on the float and began to get hammered ourselves. After downing the first bottle, Missy, who was sitting next to me, suggested we play a drinking game called "I Never" she had learned at a Rice party.

"It's easy," she said. "Whoever's turn it is makes a statement that begins with the words 'I Never.' If you've never done whatever that person says, you don't have to drink. But if you have done it, you drink."

"Give an example," Matt said.

Missy sat back on her heels, happy to be in charge. "Okay. Let's say it's my turn. I could say, 'I never made out with Johnny Ludden behind the junior high gym.' Now everyone who can honestly say they've never made out with Johnny behind the junior high gym can refrain from drinking. Rhonda, on the other hand, better make like a fish."

Rhonda turned red and buried her face in her hands, and for a moment I was sure she had quit breathing. Dub laughed so hard champagne spewed out her nose and down her EXPOSE YOURSELF TO ART T-shirt.

"I always thought Johnny was lying when he told us about all the chicks he nailed back there," Doug said, torturing poor Rhonda further.

Over the next hour I learned much about my allies. It turns out Doug and Missy had kissed in elementary school. Dub had caught her parents getting stoned on a camping trip. Matt was the only one among us who had had sex with the editor of a high school newspaper. (The rest of us were forced to admit we were still lousy with virginity. Missy *had* contemplated groupiehood in Material Issue's Econo Lodge room, but the bass player in question passed out before any deflowering had taken place.) I was surprised to learn Doug had tried out for, and been cut from, his junior high football team.

Dub upped the ante a bit with her next probe.

"I've never masturbated," she said, arching her eyebrows at her male comrades.

None of the girls drank; they just stared wide-eyed, lips pursed in tight little prunes of giddy anticipation. They broke into hysterics when Doug slugged down his André with gusto. Bill and I followed a bit more reluctantly. Noticing his little brother wasn't drinking, Bill levied his wrath against his sibling.

"Boy, I know how long you spend in the bathroom. You best start drinking." He said this in a tone I thought reserved for the chastising of black children by their parents on television sitcoms.

Matt bashfully raised his plastic chalice, and in a flash of bravado, said "Cheers" before sipping.

He was rewarded with polite, if sarcastic, golf tournament applause from the women. Doug's turn was next, and I thought surely he would settle the score with the girls. Instead, he blindsided me.

"I've never not kissed someone of the opposite sex in my life," he said.

"What kind of ass-backwards English is that?" I said. "Does that mean you have kissed every girl you've chanced upon during the past sixteen years?"

"I think what he means is that he *has* kissed a girl at least once in his life," Rhonda said, picking perhaps the most inopportune time to find her voice.

"Bingo," said Doug proudly.

No one was drinking. This was embarrassing. I turned to look out the barn door and tried to sneak a shot, but it was hopeless. I was snagged.

"Just as I suspected!" Doug bellowed. "My boy! From this day forward, your Indian warrior name is No Lips."

I wanted to explain that I had had opportunities to kiss girls. In eighth grade, Charlene "the Holstein"

Sanders towed me into a closet during my first boy/girl party, hoisted her arms over my shoulders, and tried to initiate me; but in the dark, my dodge-and-parry skills overwhelmed her power-smooch strategy. In California, a youngish receptionist at my mom's office kissed me at a staff party, but it was in front of a knot of smirking real estate agents. Besides, it was one of those "Isn't he cute? Won't he be handsome when he's a man?" sort of kisses . . . though it was on the mouth.

"I think it's sweet," Missy said, making me feel worse.

"I do too, No Lips," cooed Doug. I tried to stand but managed only an 80-degree angle before crumpling back into an all-fours stance. My only experience with alcohol had been with beer. A case of Schaeffer Light did you the courtesy of providing a glutted, anesthetized, and som-nolent sensation to warn you of oncoming drunkenness. André just snuck up and kicked your ass. My lurching induced a fresh cannonade of laughter. I heard Doug say, "And he's a lush on top of it." He sounded as if he were on another planet, as if his voice had to travel three or four seconds to reach my ears.

On my second attempt, I succeeded in standing. I grabbed the remaining bottle and chugged the dregs. Pausing to wipe champagne spittle off my chin, I announced I was leaving.

"Oh no you don't, No Lips," Dub said. "You're not driving anywhere. Give me your keys."

I'm sure I put up resistance, but not enough, because the next thing I knew, I was in the passenger seat of my car, changing eight tracks at every stoplight. Rhonda was driving, and Dub and Missy were following us to the York villa in Missy's Land Cruiser.

Don Henley was fervently warning me about life in the fast lane as we pulled into the circular, red-brick drive, but his advice went for naught. Rhonda put the El Camino in park, turned off the engine, grabbed me by the back of my neck, and began probing my larynx with her tongue. I didn't resist. I tried wiggling my own stamp licker—a chore given the incommodious chamber it was suddenly sharing. I wanted to be able to say I kissed back this time. My eyes, I realized, were wide open. In a *Teen Beat* "Rate Your Kissing" survey that sixth grader Sarah had read aloud on a car trip, I remembered hearing "eyes open" equated with frigidness. In the light supplied by the Land Cruiser pulling in behind us, I could tell Rhonda's eyes were closed.

"Call me," she said after abruptly pulling away. She tossed the keys in my lap and loped back to the idling vehicle.

San Diego, Senior Year

I bumped into Allison Kimble in the hallway on my way to English this afternoon. She asked me if I had gotten my acceptance to SDCC yet. I told her no.

"Well, I'm keeping my fingers crossed for you," she said, faking solemnity.

"Nice sweater," I said, referring to the one tied around her shoulders. I didn't intend for her to hear. She was entering her classroom.

"Nice earrings," she said without turning around.

Houston, Sophomore Year

It was rare for the astronaut and me to be home simultaneously, especially on a Sunday morning, but he was in the kitchen nuking Lean Cuisine when I staggered downstairs the following day.

"Why aren't you golfing?" I asked. Bed gnomes had

replaced my blood with battery acid and I was expecting solitude.

"Fine, thank you," he said. This was as funny as the astronaut got. He fussily pulled the plastic film off his low-cal chicken fettuccine and tossed it in the garbage can.

"Yummy-looking breakfast you got there," I said.

"I call it lunch. After one in the afternoon, the meal we have is called *lunch.*"

I had slept until one?

"I've already golfed," he continued. "I shot a seventy-nine. I appreciate your concern."

The bastard could even golf. He had taken up the sport only three years ago, and, as with most of his passions, he wouldn't quit until he mastered it. He bought the instructional videotapes. He took lessons, subscribed to *Golf Digest,* hit balls at the all-night driving range. Why couldn't he suffer a midlife crisis and buy a Corvette like all the other Clear Lake fathers? Maybe take up cliff diving—something that could really get him hurt.

I stepped around the astronaut, who was eating over the sink—the place where most of our meals were consumed at home—and opened the refrigerator door. I pulled out three tortillas, rolled them up, and devoured them sans toppings. Doug had explained to me once that tortillas, like life rafts on luxury liners, expand exponentially. Once in your stomach they search out loitering alcohol and sop it up into harmless starch mush.

"You'll never get any bigger eating that way," the astronaut said, scrutinizing me with the eye of a rancher sizing up soon-to-be-auctioned bulls.

I said nothing and plodded back toward the stairway leading to the sanctuary of my room.

"This letter from your sister has been sitting here a couple days," he said before I reached safety. I returned and took the envelope from his hand but waited until I made it to my room before opening it.

> *'sup, bro?* [One year in an ethnically diverse school and she thought she was MC Lyte.]
> *high school = cake, no problemo*
> *u/al . . . ¿all quiet on the eastern front?* [Forgive her, her style, O Lord. We let her read e. e. cummings and listen to Prince as a child.]
> *wanted 2 send enclosed school mug shot for your wallet . . . feel free 2 tell buddies i'm babe you scored in canada on fishing trip w/al . . . but u must tell me, and get names and phone numbers, if any of them say i'm hot or fine . . .* [On the back of the photo, she had written in the sissified script no male can duplicate, "stevie, u and the trout were biting, you were better"] *¿what is it w/high school? i thought every1 would b a bit < asinine . . . in student council we spent our first meeting deciding the colours* [She had mastered pretentiousness] *of the streamers for gym decoration . . . the principal said he's considering bringing drug dogs on campus and searching our lockers, yet all we can talk about is whether we should go with traditional blue and white or choose something radical like a navy blue-columbia blue combo . . . please write back with some brotherly advice.*
> [Go with the traditional blue and white, for God's sake!]
> *by the way, brother, u seem 2 have charmed a friend o' mine . . . i don't mean to be gossipy, but it appears all your late nights with god (i've*

heard all about it—no thanks 2 u) has 1 of my friends taking down her keanu reeves posters . . .
[I knew where this was heading—Rhonda must have written Sarah about me.] *¿was it your rippling pectorals as you brandished a hammer? ¿could it have been that enchanting spell u cast on defenseless maidens? ¿perhaps your beguiling nordic complexion?* [Sarah believes she governs the rotation of the planet with her punctuation. Were she ever to end a sentence with a period, time, as we know it, would freeze—her semicolons, in fact, throw off the atomic clock a smidgen.]
it could be any number of things as far as i'm concerned, stud, but something about you has dub circling prom dates on her calendar

—s

San Diego, Senior Year

Standing on tiptoes I reached for the rigid blue plastic casing of my Battleship game and pulled it down from the top shelf of my bedroom closet. I snapped open the cover and withdrew the three-inch pipe and sealed Baggie of marijuana stashed in the compartments that once housed aircraft carriers and destroyers. Stuffing the contraband in the front pocket of my cutoffs and throwing on a Dr. Zog's Sex Wax T-shirt, I traipsed out the back door and followed the trail through the dunes to the surf. I wandered a half mile down the beach, listening to the Afghan Whigs on my Discman, before plopping down on the sand. I stuffed the bowl of the pipe with what little pot I had on hand. I hadn't been smoking or buying much lately, managing an entire six-week grading period without getting busted at school. Using a trusty Bic disposable, I lit the pipe and took the first hit. Twenty minutes later I was a kite.

Midnight found me torpid, searching the Southern California night sky for a star, any star. Dub and I used to lie naked on the floor of her bedroom and study stars through the glass of her French doors.

I had gone into DeMouy's office earlier in the day to tell him I was quitting the assignment.

"Fine," he said.

"I'm serious," I said. "I really *can't* go on."

"I understand," he said.

I stood and wiped my eyes with the sand-free portion of my palm. I began walking home, soon I was jogging. By the time I could see the lights of my mother and sister's house I was sprinting. I vaulted upstairs, flipped on the Macintosh power switch, and wrote.

Houston, Sophomore Year

I don't think I've mentioned I was already in love with Dub—had been since the first day she spoke to me. I know what you're thinking: mature, true, lasting love isn't conceived in a six-minute exchange walking from geometry to world history, that what I was experiencing was some puerile infatuation. All I can tell you is that I had never felt this way about a girl before and I doubt I ever will again. The fifty-five-minute span I sat behind her every day in geometry was my primary motivation for breathing. I spent the rest of my cognizant hours conceiving one-liners like some vaudevillian hack, so I could glibly toss them into our conversations ("Mrs.

Lanigan's wearing a turtleneck to cover hickeys"). I memorized her class schedule, which had fallen like the Seventh Seal, unwadded, from her backpack pocket, resulting in a system of trails and choreography that allowed me to give her a rote nod and mouthed "hey" in yet another hallway.

The list only gets longer and increasingly pathetic. Every song on the radio had become "Ode to Us," complete with mental transference of Steve and Dub into starring roles. Daily wardrobe was screened with Dub's tastes in mind—vests, beads, bracelets, untucked tie-dyed T-shirts, battered Levi's, Doc Martens. I drove by her house. I stopped just short of carving our names in an oak tree on the village green.

I had assumed that, in long-running television series fashion, Doug and Dub's squabbling and competitiveness would escalate in such a way that their only recourse would be choosing a second and dueling or fornicating against the back wall of the gym. But with the arrival of Sarah's dispatch, I found my love requited—the morning after I'd risked mononucleosis with the object of my desire's close friend.

●●●

"I suppose if I had given you shit about your never having done heroin, you'd be playing bass for Alice in Chains by now?"

It was Doug. His phone call awakened me. I had gone back to bed immediately after reading Sarah's letter. I looked at my clock and discovered it was four in the afternoon.

"What are you talking about?" I wedged the receiver between my pillow and exposed ear, enabling me to speak with minimal use of motor skills.

"Don't be coy with me, Lips," Doug said.

"Who told you?"

"Who hasn't would be a better question . . . Rhonda's been telling everyone she sees."

"Oh boy."

"So I guess you'll be doing something with your girl-friend tonight?"

"That's not funny." My girlfriend? I had hardly ever considered Rhonda, let alone considered her my girl-friend. I was suddenly grateful I had to be at work in an hour. "Come by the theater tonight. I'll get you into something."

"That was on the agenda anyway. I'm going with Dub tonight."

I jerked up and instantly wished I had taken my time. Champagne residue, stirred by the burst of kinetic ener-gy, streamed through capillaries that had believed, in good faith, the evening's threat was over. Fresh pain in my temples and eye sockets knocked me back down to my pillow.

"Did you ask her out?" I asked.

"No, she called this morning. She asked me."

I hung up, rolled over onto my stomach, and draped one arm over the side of the bed, brushing my fingers against the marine-cropped white carpet. I surveyed the knobbed and valleyed drywall on the starboard side of my room. I imagined driving an ant-sized jeep up and down the wall's moguls. The smaller I pictured myself, the easier I disappeared and the more at peace I felt. My uniform was hanging in my closet, and I knew, momen-tarily, I would need to shower, pull my arms and head through the appropriate holes, and leave; but I couldn't will my corpse from under the comforter. Immobility, on one hand, was symptomatic of a killer hangover, and on the other, my wrestling match with a virgin emotion. The only experience I'd had with jealousy was secondhand, though I knew, by virtue of literature, jealousy had driven men into the clergy, to murder, to the French Foreign Legion, to the arms of prostitutes.

The only sensation akin to what I was feeling now had occurred when I was twelve. Mom took Sarah and me to see *Phantom of the Opera* on Broadway. During intermission, Sarah and I waited with the absently milling throng in the chandelier-lit red velvet and marble lobby while our mother went to score Cokes for us and white wine for herself. She returned incensed.

"Some boy grabbed my breasts as I was bringing our drinks back over." I couldn't tell if my mom was going to cry or go ballistic. "He had the nerve to say, 'Thank you, ma'am. The pleasure is mine.'"

I whipped my head about furiously, ready to bring the full force of my 105 pounds to bear on the miscreant.

I visualized strangling the unknown mother fondler, relishing each nanosecond it took to drain his life force. My fantasy came stocked with policemen trying vainly to pry me off the body. With my digits dug so deeply into the monster's eye sockets, the men in blue are forced to wait until I grow weak from hunger.

I was so wrapped up in my fantasy, I didn't notice the females of my tribe returning to their seats until Sarah yelled at me from ten yards ahead. My two-dimensional physique aided the body dodging required to catch up. When I'd made the family whole, Mom turned and faced us.

"There he is," she said, more to Sarah than to me. She flashed her pupils into the top right corner of her eye sockets to indicate the perpetrator was over her shoulder. A group of four tuxedoed prep schoolers had set up camp in the middle of the aisle. Without asking, I knew the guilty party. He was the one holding court; the other three were merely orbiting their leering sun. I told myself I would be the black hole that swallowed his galaxy or the supernova that vaporized him instantly. But I couldn't act. My personal gravity prevented me.

However, Sarah, keeper of the family testosterone, acted in my stead. She approached the man/boy. Smiling up at him, she interrupted his lewdly conjectural discourse on the rich, mellowed savoriness of older women, seized and extended the waistline of his slacks, and slowly poured her Coke into the gap.

"The pleasure was mine," she said to him.

Mortified security guards asked Sarah to leave, so Mom and I exited as well, though I'm certain my ten-year-old sister could have fended for herself on Broadway. As we stepped out of the theater and onto the street, Mom knelt down and held Sarah's elbows.

"Darling . . . that was the wrong boy."

"That's okay, Mom," Sarah said. "They all have it coming."

The point of my story is this: I had experienced a branch of jealous rage before. With Mom, though, I'd felt protective; my turf had been invaded. It felt only remotely like what I was suffering now, splayed out in bed considering spying on Doug and Dub from the projection booth at the movie that night.

As it was a Sunday night, odds were good Desdemona and Cassio would be attending one of the seven o'clock features. Narrowing the possibilities was simple. I eliminated both buddy cop flicks, the teen slasher sequel, the Disney rereleased animated classic, the *Saturday Night Live* spin-off (Doug and I had seen it twice already), and the latest Sharon Stone effort (management was particularly diligent in enforcing the R rating for this one). That left only the foreign coming-of-age story and a "magical romp" in which souls and bodies get switched around, resulting in hilarity and fresh understanding.

I knew I would have no trouble spotting Doug, and he didn't disappoint me later that evening. With his blond hair and baseball cap he has a beaconlike quality even without his inherent hamminess. I spied him walking backward down the aisle of the foreign film auditorium, gazing up at the windowettes. When he identified my form behind the glass, he made a cavalier bow, bending low on his left leg while extending his right leg behind him. He held his John Deere cap in his right fist which crossed his body and extended his unbent left arm parallel to the ground. He then morphed quickly from musketeer to Klingon, standing and pounding his chest twice with his fist and saluting the projection booth with his entire hand. I scanned the area behind him for Dub. My heart felt like a transplanted organ trying desperately to appease the surrounding white blood cells. She wasn't behind him. Maybe she hadn't come. Maybe she'd called and told him she would wait for me to sow my wild oats. Maybe Doug is the bearer of glad tidings. Maybe . . .

Nope. There she was.

But I had to laugh at the roster of Doug's big date. Dub was already seated, and on either side of her were Rhonda and Missy. The three of them turned in their seats to give me mock parade waves with stiff hands and rotating wrists.

Feeling a bit like Lucky, the Lucky Charms spokesleprechaun, I jigged from projector to projector clicking my heels together. My concerns, my petty jealousies, my hangover—all vanished. A knock on the metal door of my sanctum delayed my rendition of "Danny Boy."

"Steve?" The voice registered as the door cracked open: It was Rhonda.

I had forgotten one little problem. "Uh, yeah," I answered. Rhonda slunk all the way into the dimly lit booth and closed the door behind her.

"I wanted to see you, find out how you were feeling today. Doug said you sounded terrible. You had a lot to drink last night." As she spoke, Rhonda moved closer to me. I turned away and fumbled with a reel, trying desperately to look involved in a crisis centering on this renegade cog. I sat up on one of the high projectionist's stools and considered improvising a call to Hollywood to lambast some imaginary reel factory schmuck.

"Yeah, I felt like hell all day. I mostly slept," I said.

"Poor baby," she said, moving up behind me and juicing my shoulder bone sockets. We continued that way silently for a rugged minute. I felt myself spinning to face her. Damn these rotating stools!

"Let me make you feel better," she said, placing her knuckles on my thighs and leaning in for the Great Tongue Probe II. With her mouth millimeters away, I turned away. A lusty, yet quickly aborted, cheek kiss followed.

"You're really not supposed to be in here," I said flatly.

"And you're really an asshole," she said before huffing out.

●●●

As punishment for spurning her friend, Dub treated me like an immigrant from planet Dickhead. My orchestrated waves and nods were met blankly in the halls. My attempts at playing the fortune-teller game were snuffed with shushes and head shaking. On Tuesday of homecoming week, Cassandra Holbrook, the frazzled chief architect of spirit week at Grace High, broke down in class and sobbed, "People don't understand! It's hard being popular!" I waited for Dub's sickle wit to hew her asunder, but she didn't even smirk. On Wednesday I wore a tie to school—a hideous, five-inch-wide expanse of liver-colored quilted polyester emblazoned with images of soulful-eyed Great Danes. I heightened the effect with a Masonic tie tack and chain. This attracted guffaws, stares, whistles, looks of contempt from Skate or Diers. From Dub I garnered the once-over a casting agent gives to "Man Hailing Cab #147." On Friday I finally scored my first points of the week when I leaned forward and whispered in her ear, "Boy, I hope we win the big game tomorrow."

She said nothing, but from behind I saw her shoulders vibrating. She was trying to keep from laughing. Rhonda had also avoided me like the JC Penney's Young Miss fall collection, but that neglect could continue ad infinitum for all I cared.

●●●

Trey Collier had arranged his three art classes sequentially so that only a lunch period interrupted his studies. With the permission of his guru, Mr. Harley, he spent the available three-and-a-half-hour stretch in the Whiteside barn, putting finishing touches on *Get Hammered.* Most of that time was spent gluing Life Savers on the overhanging cardboard eaves we had tacked along the bed part of the flatbed truck. Those of us with no artistic training were put in charge of organizing the candies by color. We knew we wanted the Life Savers to spell out "Grace Order of Dadaists say . . . ," but there had been lively tête-à-têtes about what the final word would be. Late on Thursday night Trey reached an executive decision, and, relying on the menu from his Chinese takeout, completed the slogan with the Chinese symbol for *pork.*

Beverly as truck owner and Trey as chief designer earned the coveted *Get Hammered* driver and navigator positions. The rest of us would watch the parade together. On homecoming day, Doug moved through the lines of floats with all the arrogance of a jockey set to ride Secretariat. The sponsor of the student council used a bullhorn to tell the drivers to start their engines. As we were wishing Beverly and Trey luck, Tom Pittman approached Doug.

"What does that say?" he said, pointing at the Chinese word for *pork*. He was concerned, presumably, because we had used three times the number of Life Savers—and orange rather than lime ones at that—on the initials of our group's name. Hence, the slogan "Grace Order of Dadaists says Pork" read more like "GOD says X."

Our leader answered without hesitation, "Beat the Mustangs."

Within twenty minutes, the dozen remaining members of GOD had carved out a two-row-by-six-seat section of prime parade viewing turf in the football grandstands. Those who could separate me from Dub had successfully done so. I sat on the aisle in row two; she took the innermost seat of row one. Even Rhonda was willing to sit one seat closer to me, immediately to Dub's left. I had begun to lose faith in Sarah's letter. What if she had meant to write Rhonda's name and absentmindedly substituted Dub's?

Doug, sitting beside me, chin in hand, grunted.

"Can't they do any better than that?" he said, pointing to the first row where a full score of Skate or Diers were holding newspapers, upside down, in front of their faces in showy indifference to the parade beginning to take shape on the track before them. Though I was confident Doug harbored no regrets about the direction GOD had taken, part of him longed for the abject loathing Skate or Die inspired. He knew the satire we intended with *Get Hammered* would pass harmlessly over the heads of most of his peers.

As organizers of the parade, the student council was automatically given lead position, and I admit I was impressed, from a strictly aesthetic point of view, with their float. Given the demographics of the community who gravitated to student government, it was hardly surprising that they found it within their quasi-pontifical reach to obtain a genuine yacht. They had affixed a Styrofoam shell to the outside and painted it a mottled greenish brown, approximating the scabby, barnacled look of a pirate ship. A skull-and-crossbones-emblazoned sail hung from the mast, and a legion of blond, Soloflex-buffed pirates with eyepatches, bandannas, and stuffed parrots wired to their shoulders manned battle stations. The boat was skirted by a patch of ocean blue-painted plywood. A horse head (which, for me at least, evoked *The Godfather* more readily than our gridiron rivals) stuck out of the ersatz sea. As the float rounded the curve and came into full view of the student body, the band broke into "Bucs Fight." The Buccaneer Babes began their synchronized Rockette routine in the stands, and the cheerleaders kicked their heels backward and jabbed pom-poms heavenward each time the band paused for a shouted chorus of "Bucs Fight! Bucs Fight! Yay, Bucs Fight!" The game jersey-clad football players slouched in folding chairs facing the student body on the inside of the track. The deities-in-waiting feigned aplomb, succeeding only in looking as bored as the Skate or Diers whose asses they were silently vowing to kick Monday at school.

Doug had drawn number 16 in the parade order lottery, which meant *Get Hammered* represented the midpoint of the parade. For a group that took special pride in its skepticism, we young GODs were certainly being blatantly unblasé waiting for our entry to arrive, sniping at the more garish efforts of our competitors (except for Lynnette, who apparently expected the Second Coming to occur on one of the passing flatbed trucks) and trying to top each other with the most fatuously generic cheer. Veg won that battle, based at least partially on the way his voice cracked and went falsetto when he stood during a lull between floats to howl with insane gusto, "Go, team!" Doug kept standing to bellow, "Pork!" Virginia and Zipper sat below me trying to decide who was the cutest of the mohawked Skate and Diers, a discussion that I yearned not to overhear.

Matt Whiteside, still enough of a Boy Scout to bring binoculars, was the first to spot the pride of GOD as it turned off Spruce Terrace onto Buccaneer Boulevard.

"Thar she blows!" he announced, getting his nautical allusions mixed up.

"Is the hammer working?" his concerned brother asked.

"Aye, matey."

For perhaps the only time, GOD followed the lead of Lynnette, who was the first of our group to stand as our dadaistic masterpiece passed in front of the student body. We applauded every bit as madly as the Key Club had for their "Buccaneer Slaying Mustang," the Future Farmers for their "Buccaneer Slaying Mustang," the French Club for their "Boucanier Massacre le Cheval" or the PETA group for their "Buccaneer Domesticating Mustang." Trey, riding shotgun, gave a thumbs-up to our delirious section. In my euphoria, I failed, momentarily, to monitor the reaction of the homecoming crowd. But I quickly realized that the stunned reception *Get Hammered* was reaping justified every sweltering, Life-Saver-gluing minute spent in the Whiteside barn.

The band, section by section, simply quit playing. Dancing cheerleaders, puzzled by the silence, turned to face *Get Hammered*. Several dropped their pom-poms. Skate or Diers lowered their newspapers. Administrators stood transfixed by the motorized contraption before them. Waves of students and teachers turned to stare at our bantam cheering section, effectively cowing us into silence. After what seemed like an hour, the hush was unexpectedly broken by a lone bass drum, which began to boom in time with the downward stroke of our hammer. Again and again the drummer punctuated the hammer's "impact," providing a slow but ominous-sounding rhythm. Then, one of the football players began clapping with the beat. He was joined by the rest of the team, and soon the entire grandstand had fallen in line, giving the pep rally the aura of a Celtic funeral march. Our float had passed completely from view before the drum major whistled the band back into the Grace fight song to accompany the Ski Club's "Buccaneer Slaying Mustang"—modified by their radical substitution of a ski pole for the traditional cutlass.

San Diego, Senior Year

I got my third letter from Doug today. If I don't start writing back I'm sure I'll lose all contact with Texas. That might not be a bad thing. I'm always afraid to open his letters for fear I will learn fresh details of *her* life. I guess that since I've been writing for DeMouy, and I've had to type her name regularly, I've grown a bit more accustomed to it. But all my information is old. I don't want to know what she's up to now, unless maybe it's something tragic.

> *Lip Monster!*
>
> *Forget everything you've read. It's still possible to have sex in college. Cheap, tawdry, meaningless, fleeting, dirty, anonymous sex. You can't have it with anyone, but no one stops you from taking matters into your own hand.*
>
> *You ought to come here for college. Austin has to be the coolest city in Texas. Even the frat boys*

recycle. After my Friday Chem II class, our T.A.
takes us out and buys us pitchers of Shiner Bock
at The Crown and Anchor. [Shiner Bock is like
water in Austin.]

 I'm drumming for a band now. I answered an
ad that was tacked up in the student union build-
ing. It was the only band that didn't want to play
lame-ass white funk/rap. Get this . . . we're called
the Originals and we play only 1970s guitar rock.
Just as you always predicted, I'm out there resur-
recting "Sweet Home Alabama." We've been open-
ing up on weeknights at the perfectly named Hole
in the Wall. It's right here on the Drag. We've
started drawing pretty well, and we've been
promised a weekend night pretty soon.

 Hang in there, buddy. Remember, the thighs
of Texas are upon you.
Hook 'em! (God, I'm spirited.)
Doug

Houston, Sophomore Year

The school official who dictated that our fifty-dollar prize for most original float was to be deposited directly into our school account displayed a wisdom rare among his ilk, as I'm sure the loot would have been squandered on beer had we received cash in hand. When Principal B. J. Stokes stammered "The Grace Order of Dadaists" as winner of the "most original" category, its cynical membership reacted with all the reserve associated with English soccer fans. We hugged; we pumped our fists in Jimmy-Connors-march-to-the-U.S.-Open-semis fashion; we screamed, "Pork!"

 In the melee I found myself pushed next to Dub. We

studied each other for a pregnant few seconds. I would have stood there with a Gomer Pyle expression on my face for days, but she spread her arms, inviting me within. I stepped forward and wrapped my arms farther around her than celebratory etiquette allows, gaining the opposite side of her back with each hand. As she turned her head sideways and pressed her ear against my collarbone, I felt sure Sarah's letter *had* been accurate: Dub felt *something* for me, maybe a fraction of what I felt for her, but in some form, we had connected.

Suddenly I felt a Viking slap on my back. I withdrew from the hug and turned to find Doug ripe for manly celebrating. His fists were clenched overhead in a V for victory sign, and he was crooning the opening lines of "We Are the Champions." Immediately aware of the creature from the blue jean lagoon testing the metal of my zipper, I jammed my fists into my pockets and joined in. We didn't get very far before the band struck up the alma mater. This put me in the awkward position of trying to decide whether or not to take my hands out of my pockets to put my arms around my neighbors, as convention dictated for the rendering of the song. Doug was similarly perplexed for dissimilar reasons: Meekly joining in this maudlin tribute to an institution for which he acknowledged no fealty whatever was just too hypocritical to contemplate. Evidently misconstruing my woody-concealment gesture as a show of defiance, he also stuck his hands in his pockets, and the two of us finished off the Queen song to the tune of "Hail Grace High."

San Diego, Senior Year

Toby the Party, so named for his talent for knowing the location of every kegger in Greater San Diego, offered me a couple shots of tequila on my way in from the parking lot after lunch. Toby had served as sort of the stoner Welcome Wagon when I first arrived in town. I wouldn't exactly call him a friend, but we had cut plenty of classes together.

"You got the new Mudhoney CD yet?" T. P. inquired as he pulled a lime out of his glove box. I shook my head no. Toby's big dream, practically the only thing he talked about, was moving to Seattle once he got out of school, growing his hair down to his knees, and playing in the grungiest band he could find.

I took the second shot he offered out of guilt for not seeing much of Toby lately. Despite feeling a bit sloppy afterward, I stopped by DeMouy's office. The evening before I had found a used cassette called *Spooky Sounds and Naughty Noises* at Play It Again Sam's. I thought DeMouy could probably punch it in on Halloween. Besides, it only cost me a buck.

Allison Kimble, however, occupied my all-but-branded chair. On her lap she held open a massive organizer/planner. I scanned it from the doorway. Every day appeared to have four or five entries. DeMouy was sifting through files, gathering materials Allison must have requested.

"Have you gotten the application from ITT Tech that I asked for?" I asked in my Clear Lake–honed Thurston Howell voice. DeMouy didn't respond, but he smiled slightly without looking up from the files.

Allison swiveled. "Well, if it isn't Bandanna Man."

And it occurred to me, *What the hell am I doing here? Can't I see all the disturbing parallels?* Without thinking of an appropriate exit line, I closed the door, walked out to my car, and drove to the beach. I had enough school for the day.

Houston, Sophomore Year

Stan Jr., Doug's nearly legal-aged older brother, proved to be the hero of the night. It took him only three 7-Elevens to find a convenience store lackey willing to sell him a case of Busch.

"I'm just glad I could do something to help American kids," he said, dropping Doug and me off at the Whiteside barn. We were compelled to meet on Homecoming Eve to dismantle *Get Hammered*; Beverly's parents needed the truck the following day. Doug and I weren't the only two who thought demolition work could only improve with beer. Most of the members showed up with smuggled bottles stuck in baggy jeans pockets, hidden in purses, tucked in boots.

Veg brought his parents' video camcorder and recorded the evening's merriment. Matt started up the hammer and all of us climbed aboard the float. Veg set the camera on the hood of Zipper's convertible Rabbit and joined us in the shot. We replaced the standard teeth-revealing "cheese" with the less gummy, but more germane, "Pork." Later Doug suggested Veg shoot Matt and me forcing him like a prisoner, in affected slow motion, to the spot near the truck's cab where the hammer struck regularly. Veg, sensing his president's intentions, stopped the tape just before Doug pulled his head out of the killing zone. Doug took the camera out of Veg's hands and shot a couple of seconds from the vantage point of the truck cab as the hammer swung toward him. Handing the camera back to Veg, he ran across the barn to the shelf where we had stored our leftover tempera paint. He grabbed a bottle of the red we used on the handle, unscrewed the top, and poured it across the cab of the truck, letting it spill down the back in rivulets. Then he positioned Veg in his original taping spot.

"Okay, Veg. When I say action, you start recording." Doug motioned for Matt and me to rejoin him. He pulled his sweatshirt up so his head was covered, then instructed us to grab him by the arms. He positioned himself so that his back blocked the still-runny red paint from the camera. As the hammer began its descent, Doug shouted action.

When the hammer struck, Doug flailed his headless body backward revealing the faux blood stain where, through the magic of video, there had once been a skull. He then plowed through a half case, or "twack" (our contraction of "twelve pack"), while watching his videotaped execution over and over again. Consequently, he wasn't much help in taking apart the float. (Of course, even if he'd been sober, Doug probably still wouldn't have been much help.)

We left the retained heat of the barn for the woven-rubber-tubing lawn chairs scattered randomly outside the huge swinging doors. A cool, but clammy, Gulf breeze rewarded us for the completion of our project.

Rhonda's attention to Matt Whiteside in the ensuing hours was so blatant I was a bit embarrassed to be sitting four lawn chairs away. Matt didn't appear to be aware of her fawning, or at least he didn't mind it. If she were stalking Matt in hopes of provoking me, she was succeeding only in easing whatever residual guilt I felt over . . . well, over letting her kiss me, I guess. Dub must have been equally aware of Rhonda's translucence, because when Rhonda said she wanted to see Matt's aquarium-confined tarantula, Dub hacked up the swig of Busch she had just taken.

Bill was stretched out on a deck chair with Holly curled across his lap. Her arm was around his neck and his hand rested on her hip. The two were representing the Grace Jesters Drama Club and the journalism department, respectively, in the following night's homecoming court festivities. Lynnette, skittish as usual, was interrogating the couple about the event, which was, by then, only twenty hours away.

"But won't y'all just freak if they call your names? What if one of you wins and has to dance with someone else, won't you just freak? Does the gym really look like a tropical paradise? Do you know what you're going to wear?" Lynnette catechized rapid-fire with visions of *Cinderella* in her head.

Holly did her best to respond patiently before Lynnette interrupted with her next question. I was glad Doug had passed out. Had he been sentient, I'm afraid he would have excommunicated Lynnette for such unabashed false convention-worshipping.

"All they do to turn the gym into a tropical paradise is put up three or four fake palm trees, bring in a little tiki hut to serve punch out of, and, oh yeah, they give you plastic leis as you walk in the door," Holly said.

"Imagine how long boys can joke about 'getting leied' at the door," Missy added.

"I want to go," Dub said, startling those assembled, Lynnette excepted.

"I think you *should* go." All the heads that had turned to stare at Ms. Varner swiveled toward Samantha, who was speaking. "Well, why not? You can't really just sit back and laugh at teenagers in their natural habitat your whole life unless you've done some clinical research."

"Sure you can," Missy said. "That's why we have John Hughes movies—so we *don't* actually have to go to high school dances."

Dub jutted out her lower lip and blew her hair out of her eyes before explaining.

"It's not that I need to see kids puking in the parking lot or middle-aged teachers in kimonos hosing down couples on the dance floor to be able to laugh at them," Dub explained. "I just want to go to at least one dance, see what it feels like to get dressed up, maybe wear makeup, introduce a boy to my parents, watch him fidget on my front porch. I want the whole Hallmark-Card-Norman-Rockwell-American-rite-of-passage thing. It's a life experience I've never had. And it sucks to realize I probably never will."

I wondered briefly how much Dub had had to drink but was restored to the present from my mental score-carding of the night's consumption by sharp taps on my Doc Martens. Samantha, sitting perpendicular to me, was signaling me by kicking my foot. I tried to read the senior's face, but her back was to the open barn doors. All I saw was silhouette.

"Double U, sometimes I don't understand you," Missy said. "Getting your wisdom teeth out is a 'life experience,' "—Missy made the international quote mark sign with her fingers—"but you don't see people paying a cover charge to get into the dentist's office. I swear, you are the only person I know who makes decisions based on what will provide the best material for a diary."

"It's too late to care about it now, anyway. Shockingly enough, nobody's asked me to go with them," Dub said.

Veg, Zipper, and Virginia left together shortly after midnight in Veg's Volkswagen bus. I asked them for a ride, as both Doug and I were carless, but Dub volunteered to take us home. The move elicited a lip-parted head swivel from Rhonda and a smirk from Missy, who'd had surprisingly little to say all evening. Missy, though, was the driver and I accepted the offer despite the prospect of occupying close quarters with the doubly spurned Rhonda.

Matt, Missy, Bill, and I served as pallbearers for the

comatose Doug Chappell. As we carried his limp body to the cargo space of Missy's Land Cruiser, Dub followed, genuflecting, sprinkling warm spittle from a Busch empty, and speaking in near-Latin, *"In nominee padre, et fille . . ."*

As it turned out, Rhonda ended up riding home with Lynnette. I climbed in the backseat of Missy's forest-green status symbol, and Missy and Dub got in front. We pulled out of the private road leading up to the Whiteside ranch and onto Farm Road 1212. Missy cracked her window open electronically and punched in her cigarette lighter.

"Deary," Dub said, "smoking is so eighth grade."

Ignoring Dub, Missy tapped a Merit out of a pack in her purse. "So, Barney, how are we going to get Otis here safely into bed?"

I glanced behind me. A drool puddle had formed under Doug's mouth. "We can't really count on Doug helping us out. I need to get ahold of Stan Jr. He could take care of him. I won't be able to deactivate their home security alarm."

Missy reached into the glove box, pulled out a cellular phone, and waved it blindly into the backseat. "If this doesn't work, I say we just leave the video he made tonight on their front doorstep with a note saying, 'I asked for a *kidney*-shaped pool, damn it!' "

I dialed the Chappell "children's line." Thankfully, twenty-year-old Stan Jr., answered, though he spoke a language understood only by those awakened from a deep sleep.

"Gorrdom ssshh bagror?" he said. His inflection rose at the end of his greeting, so I was pretty sure he meant it as a question.

"Stan, it's Steve. Can you meet me at your front door in about ten minutes? Doug is pretty messed up."

"Doog gnik cufeb rette bsiht," he grumbled before hanging up.

Pulling up in front of the Chappells' red-clay-shingled Spanish-style hacienda, I was relieved to find Stan had at least partially understood my plea. Doug's sibling was spread-eagled on his back on the front lawn, asleep. His robe was untied, revealing a pair of Mickey Mouse–adorned boxers. A pubic hair exhibition was visible through the open fly of his shorts.

"Now, this is classy," Missy said as she turned off the engine. "Kind of kindles all my maternal fires."

I hopped out and closed Stan's robe before shaking his shoulder. Stan struggled to stand up.

"What happened to Boy Wonder?" Stan slurred, though he was looking at the two unfamiliar girls dragging his sibling out of the Land Cruiser.

"Twack attack," I answered.

Stan scratched his blond stomach hair and grinned. "Did he ever tell you about the drum set he got when he was thirteen?" I shook my head. "He played it every Saturday morning. Mom was happy that he showed so much dedication. What she didn't know was that the son of a bitch was only playing because he knew I'd come in wasted the night before." Stan walked over to where Dub and Missy had propped up Doug against Stan's Toyota. He took Doug's chin in his hand and used his thumb and index finger to force a lunatic smile on his brother's face. "Tomorrow your ass is mine, little brother."

Stan, as ventriloquist, nodded Doug's head and manipulated his lips.

"Yes, sir," my automated friend responded.

Stan then supplanted Dub on Doug's right side. I moved to take Missy's place, but she waved me off. "Think how it will horrify him if I can describe the inside of his room. Maybe I'll leave my purse and act offended when he can't remember me being there."

Wrapping Doug's arms around their necks, Missy

and Stan made slow progress toward the house. As they disappeared inside, I realized I was alone with Dub.

"Tomorrow will be a day Doug will remember," Dub said, breaking the silence that I perceived as awkward within seconds of our companions' departure. Dub was still looking in the direction of the open front door. I took the liberty of staring at her profile. I knew before looking that she wasn't beautiful. Her face had a cartoon puggishness to it, like an animated character smacked with a frying pan—the eyes huge and splayed at dolphin width. Separately her features would have seemed comical; together they gave her a funkiness that caught your attention like a log cabin in Genericwood Estates. Though I could see only one eyebrow from my angle, I had often noted how they harmonized her stray features. They were dark brown, her original hair color, and they arched and descended like a designer's French curve—striking and perfect.

Dub's body was an enigma. All of her clothes seemed purchased with an all-star wrestler in mind. A voyeur would have a better chance of spying Dub's mystery flesh through the gaping arm holes of one of her short-sleeved shirts than other traditional cleavage opportunities. Dub shunned more feminine garments neither out of a need to hide weight nor latent lesbian masculinity. "Comfort" was the one-word answer she would give to explain her fashion sense, but I think she was savvy enough to oblige the masses to deal with her on her own terms. Spiral perm her and dress her at the Limited and she would have evaporated in the halls of Grace.

I saw the light in Doug's upstairs room come on. Belatedly and poetically, I realized why Samantha had been kicking me earlier. She had seen Dub and me hugging. She knew Dub wanted to go to the homecoming dance. Steve, thy name is rube.

I frantically rummaged my wit for suitably ambiguous, noncommittal (read, "safe") methods of asking Dub to the homecoming dance—avenues that offered retreat and reduced the risk of rejection, double entendres like "I can't tell you how much fun the homecoming dance sounds" or "Imagine not going to the dance." I considered tossing out "I've got tomorrow night off and nothing to do," like a bucketful of fish innards on a shark safari.

My best move would have been to drink my share of the beer at the Whiteside barn, but that was an option no longer open to me. My inhibitions were still cruelly intact, and my tongue felt like a two-dollar hunk of salted beef jerky.

Instead, with each frittered second, I confirmed my wusshood. My palms were swamps and my heart that of a speed freak. When at last I had chosen words, I found I was unable to speak. I had to relinquish control of my motor skills to my spinal column. My brain became merely a terrified observer. The sound I made, however, didn't come out in the form of a sentence; I squeaked.

Dub heard, though, and turned around to face me. "Did you say something?" she asked.

I could only listen in horror as my fearless reflexive system assumed control.

"Are you looking for someone to take you to the dance tomorrow night?" my mouth asked.

"You are pathetic," she said, emphasizing all three words. "What the hell does that mean—'Are you looking for someone to take you to the dance?'" Dub paused and shook her head slowly before driving home another stake. "Is that your coy way of asking me out, or are you wondering if we should have Missy drop me off somewhere on Westheimer to go on a manhunt?"

"Forget it," I said. Missy was bounding out of the house, but she hesitated when she sensed the contention.

"No. Tell me what you meant. I mean, I already confessed to wanting to go. Were you making sure I wasn't lying?"

By now I was embarrassed and wanted to bail, but Dub had blocked my retreat. I stood there with my head bowed. This should have been easy. I couldn't even ask a girl to a dance who had not only said she desired to attend, but had also spoken affectionately of me.

"Look, can we talk about this some other time?" I said after lengthy silence assured me Dub wasn't about to let me off the hook just because we had an audience.

"No time like the present," she said.

I contemplated the likely postrejection results of this encounter. I would abandon all hope of a life colored by passion or meaning. I would melt into the blue-and-gold-painted halls of Grace, trade up to an invisible Accord, join the Future Teachers. No one would ever see me again. But now I would face my destiny like a man. I raised my head and spoke evenly.

"Dub, please go to the homecoming dance with me."

Missy raised her eyebrows, unaware this had been the theme. For one of the two times I would ever witness, Dub seemed unsure of herself. She glanced snappishly about. It occurred to me: She had expected me to back out. In fact, I think she tried to push me to it. Relief hit me even before she responded. The balance had shifted in my favor. I had made Dub nervous.

San Diego, Senior Year

Guess what. There was an ugly scene at the dinner table caused by one of the York children tonight, and I wasn't involved in it at all. I didn't say a word during the entire exchange.

Mom and Chuck cooked together. This was one of their less gross joint pursuits. Believe me, in my book, it ranked way above jogging together in matching sweat suits or French-kissing in public. This night they prepared a barbecued salmon and corn on the cob. After three years of microwaving my own meals, I tried not to miss much home cooking. I think I'm even starting to put on some significant weight. Anyway, we sat down to eat at the picnic table on the deck, and as with most discussions at home, Sarah and Mom did most, if not all, of the talking. Sarah had a new boyfriend and Mom was curious.

"But why haven't we met him?" she asked.

"He's got an internship at KPIX. He wants to get into radio after he graduates. He's always working," Sarah answered.

"Well, he must make quite a bit of money as much as he works."

"It's an internship, Mom. You don't make money at an internship; you work for free. It's the only way you can get experience in radio."

"When do you ever get to see him?"

"That's something I wanted to talk to you about."

Chuck snuck in a request for the butter, which I was happy to provide.

Sarah continued. "Danny's asked me to the Pearl Jam concert next month. He got free tickets through work."

"That's terrific. Pearl Jam's huge," said my mother, indicating the band must have made the cover of *People*.

"Yeah, but the concert's in LA. At the Forum. And nobody wants to try to drive home afterward. The plan is to get a hotel room and crash, then drive back in the morning. There are eight of us going."

"Were you planning on asking permission?"

"That's what I'm doing now."

"You expect me to let you get a hotel room with a boy? A boy I've never even met? I don't think so. Sometimes I think you think you're much older than you really are."

Chuck and I continued eating, heads down.

"God, Mom, you make it sound like we'd be acting out *Caligula* in the room. There'd be eight of us in there. I don't think anybody will be parading around naked. We'll leave the vibrators and goats here at home."

"Don't talk to me like I'm being a frump about this. Do parents today normally let their children go to concerts in the big city and stay in hotel rooms afterward?"

"No, Mom . . . just the smart ones."

I sensed Sarah had just crossed some line with this one.

"Watch it, young lady."

"It *is* smarter. Would you rather we drive back sleepy? Some people in the group might be drinking. It's just better that we stay in Los Angeles."

"Will you be one of the ones drinking?"

"Mooommm, puhleeease! You wouldn't keep Steve from going . . . and he's been known to"— long pause — "drink occasionally."

"He's eighteen, honey, and, besides, we're not talking about Steve right now." Mom turned toward her husband. She touched his forearm. "Chuck, do you think this sounds like a good idea?"

Chuck looked up reluctantly. He wearily faced his stepdaughter. "Sarah, I think your mother has a point. It doesn't sound very proper to me."

"Who cares what *you* think?" Sarah said. "*You* aren't

my father." My sister threw her napkin on her plate, left the table, and stormed out the front door. We listened to her Subaru squeal out onto Shoreline Drive.

"Is she going to eat that?" I said, pointing to her salmon.

Houston, Sophomore Year

Dub never did tell me yes. She just said to pick her up at nine. Neither of us spoke on the drive to my house. The silence forced me to consider what I had done. For the first time in my life, I had asked a girl on a date, a real date, none of this, "My friends will be there. Why don't you and your friends show up?" scammy bullshit. In doing so, I committed myself to attend a semiformal high school dance, one that, four hours ago, I had no desire to attend . . . and for good reason.

First of all, I don't dance. Outside of a couple feeble *Club MTV* imitations in front of the sliding mirror doors of my closet, I was lacking practical boogie experience. More important, to my employer, I was supposed to work homecoming night at the Cineplex. I had already alienated the other two projectionists by requesting so many nights off to work on *Get Hammered*. Third, I had not worn my suit since eighth grade. Sarah and I had been roughly the same size back then; I towered over her now. Fourth, the astronaut was home most Saturday nights, a six-hour gap each week he had, so far, been unable to fill. His married friends were locked into bridge leagues, family nights, and whatnot. Dub may want classic dating rites, but I could do without the beaming old man slipping me a fiver while imparting fatherly dos and don'ts. Last, the El Camino was sufficient for tooling around, getting my books and me to school, and transporting me to work, but not for taking a girl, presumably in a dress, to a semi-formal dance. As we turned left on Briar Cove, Missy broke the silence.

"Oh boy. You two should be the life of the party tomorrow," Missy said. Still, neither of us spoke. She continued a bit more sympathetically. "From what I hear, no one stays at the dance very long. They show up. They get their pictures taken. That way they can prove to their parents that they made it and that all the money they had demanded was necessary. Then they go to parties where everyone does the cocaine and X they bought with embezzled mum and limo money."

Missy stopped at the same spot in my driveway where she and Dub had viewed the seduction of Steve a week ago. I hoped the same image didn't flash in Dub's head. I reached for the door handle, prepared to depart without further notice, but Dub turned in her seat and told me her phone number.

"Call me tomorrow," she told me. "Do you think you can remember the number? Do you want me to write it down?"

But of course I knew it by heart.

San Diego, Senior Year

I found a postcard worthy of a missive to Doug at a trashy beachfront souvenir shop. The shop is next door to my latest haunt, Cap's. Cap's has cashed in on America's java mania. The hand-painted driftwood sign that hangs outside depicts a squinting, pipe-smoking coffee bean wearing a skipper's cap and a yellow rain slicker. I'm not sure if "Cap" is a diminutive of *cappuccino* or an extension of the sea-farin' motif established by the cartoon. A hybrid, I suppose.

I generally hit Cap's right after school. I see no one from school there. That's essential.

It's good for me to be out of the local misdemeanor-level drug ring in the late afternoon. More of us get high, or make plans to get high, at that time than any other. School just provides a convenient meeting ground. DeMouy must have made a mistake in assigning me all this writing. Instead of coming to terms with what happened back in Texas, I'm realizing how sorry my life is here. Or was this his intention? I'm more a hermit now than ever. I have to start being honest with myself. I have no friends in San Diego. I have people I party with . . . it's not the same thing.

Most of my afternoon co-sippers at Cap's are either professionals or grad students from UCSD. I made the mistake of coming in one night after ten. I was run out by college sophomores smoking clove cigarettes, strumming out-of-tune acoustic guitars, and reading free verse poetry heavy with metaphorical digressions.

I'm still a novice at my newest vice, coffee. I swallow three or four gulps of it, straight and black, barely hiding my grimace. Then I douse it with cream and thicken it with sugar. I do this when I believe no one is looking. The bottom of my mug becomes a tan sludge. Caffeine gives me such a different buzz than dope. By what factor I used to return home more mellow, I can't even begin to guess.

Anyway, back to the postcard I bought for Doug. Jason Priestley graced its front side. He looked into the camera earnestly. His chest was bare and glycerin spritzed, and his thumbs were hooked inside the waistband of his jeans. I felt dirty buying it, like I was picking up my monthly copy of *Sizzlin' Sir Loins* from Pleasure Tyme Newsstand. I didn't wuss out, though. I didn't tell the checkout guy that it was

for my little sister or that it was a joke or anything like that.
I modified the card by adding a balloon aimed at Priestley's
thin lips. "Doug, we'll always have Lubbock," Jason confessed. On the back I wrote . .

Ma mere n'est pas morte.
[*We had both read Camus'* The Stranger *in Sky's
class.*]
And neither am I.
*Texas is just a big black hole that I haven't
allowed myself to get sucked back into.
Unfortunately, you're not far from ground zero.
I'm glad to hear you're drumming. I hope Neil
Young will remember, southern men don't need
him around, anyhow.*
Rock on!
Steve

Houston, Sophomore Year

The astronaut and I had effectively negated the preserva-
tional role of "family"— food gathering, predator thwart-
ing, values establishing, weather dancing. As best as we
could, we interacted through Post-it notes and paper-
clipped currency. We didn't sink to the clichéd line painted down the middle of the house, preferring to utilize a
complicated schedule decreeing when the house could
be considered our own. The elder York was welcome to
the pre-8 A.M. hours. He had my blessing to lord over the
manor then as he saw fit. On school days my alarm clock
jolt coincided with the old man's motorized bicycle chain
wrenching open the garage doors to emancipate his
Lincoln. Of course, I didn't get up with the first static/
grunge of KTRU, Rice's weak-signaled alternative radio

station. I allowed myself two blissful snooze button slaps.

Monday through Friday were so masterfully executed that we had managed complete five-day stretches without a single nonpenned word passing between us. Weekends were normally sticky; football season made it worse. The astronaut could park himself on one of our two practical chairs and watch State U battle Other State Tech all day. He would sit there with a bowl of grapes and a liter bottle of Evian, unconcerned with who was playing. There was a time I can remember when Saturday mornings meant a comfy denful of jet fighter pilots, swilling Budweiser and wolfing down fatty toothpicked hors d'oeuvres served by Mom. The room would erupt from time to time and I would spot the patriarch laughing and backslapping almost like he was human.

When the alarm buzzed for the third time, I made it up—8:30 on a Saturday morning, an hour that I hadn't experienced in a vertical position since Christmas morning sometime in the mid-eighties. I showered, didn't shave (it wasn't a full moon), and sat down at my desk with a notepad and pen. I jotted down a twenty-eight-item Things to Do list, before adding as the twenty-ninth, *call Dub and cancel.* Then I crumpled up the list. I rocked back in my folding chair, tapping my nose with the pen cap suctioned to my tongue, and reconsidered. I could scratch *dance lessons*—not enough time. Eliminating *hotwire convertible Beamer* was probably also a wise move from both a penal and scheduling perspective. Flattening the crumpled legal sheet, I rescanned my list and found more nonessential steps I could cross out.

- BUY PIZZA-SIZED MUM WITH *"Steve and Wanda"* SPELLED IN GLUE AND GLITTER DOWN THE HANGING STREAMERS.

- SIPHON GASOLINE TO "NOT QUITE ENOUGH TO GET HOME" LEVEL.
- GET HAIR "DONE."

Soon I had the list pared down to the bare necessities.

- WAKE UP DOUG AND GIVE HIM SHIT.
- LIE TO ASTRONAUT.
- GET OFF WORK.
- AVOID DANCE FLOOR.
- SQUEEZE ZITS.

I figured I'd give Doug a reprieve and start with item two. I wrapped a bathrobe around me, depressed a bit by the olympic-ring-sized loops left after tying the belt. I padded downstairs. The astronaut sat in the stage-right chair. His feet were on the glass coffee table and the *Houston Chronicle* was on the rug beside the chair in neatly folded sections. On the screen, two Ivy League schools simulated a football game. The astronaut was dressed in his Saturday play clothes: khaki slacks, black knit golf shirt, brown Top-Siders. He was, naturally, showered and dressed for the day. He didn't look surprised to see me, though he did glance at his watch.

"Are you planning to go to the game tonight?" the astronaut asked, and I don't think I'm mistaken in adding the adverb *hopefully*.

"Which game?" I asked, genuinely confused. I pulled wet bangs out of my eyes.

"Grace and Memorial . . . your homecoming game," the astronaut said before switching his attention back to the set. He began flipping through the channels that might be carrying meaningful contests.

"Oh, that's right," I said, trying to sound interested.

"I can't. I've got to work." I walked over and occupied the other chair. I also kept my attention on the television. "Do you think I can borrow the Lincoln tonight? My car is making some funky noise."

"If you could have waited until you got back to Texas, we could have found you something more reliable," the astronaut said.

I knew I would be subjecting myself to this lecture, but I also figured that, while gloating, his mood would be such that he would relent enough to loan me his supertanker. We sat there for a few minutes, silently playing a patience game. Finally he instructed me to fill the Lincoln with gas before I brought it home. I thanked him, then counted to one hundred before excusing myself and leaving him alone in front of the television.

I spent the next hour in front of my bathroom mirror on a blackhead search and destroy mission. The assignment was treacherous. Squeeze one before it's properly aged and you end up with a pinball stuck just inside your cheek. Allow one to fester and you learn on a midnight trip to the men's room that your face resembles Pompeii. Concluding the job with a Q-Tip and alcohol rubdown, I skipped the standard intermission for the red pinchy marks on my face to return to uniform paleness, confident I would run into neither Winona Ryder nor Dub before I regained an unscourged look.

Next I rummaged through my closet, eventually emerging with a tweed, elbow-patched sports coat bought either before I had a say in clothing or under a mistaken impression that girls went for academics. I tried it on nevertheless. My forearms emerged like loaves of French bread from the sleeves—passable if I wanted to sing for a slightly bookish rockabilly band. Sighing, I examined my assembled footwear: one size nine purple Chuck Taylor, one green size ten (Doug had a pair just like it), my Docs, and a stiff pair of Mom-purchased Hush Puppies. I heard the phone ring but decided to let the astronaut answer it. The only person I could imagine calling me was comatose. Moving from shoes to shirts, I perused the three-item collection of long-sleeved pinstriped dress shirts. All had been bought predivorce. The astronaut and I didn't go malling together very often. Just then, the old man barked.

"Steve," he shouted as if addressing a private. He made my name seem shorter than its lone syllable.

"I'll get it up here," I yelled back. I picked up the body of the phone in my left hand and held the receiver to my mouth with my right still posing in the mirror.

"So what are you going to wear?" It was my sister, the psychic.

"How'd you know?" I began, though it was a stupid question.

"I just got off the phone with her. You really shocked her last night. She didn't think you would ever come around. Not a very romantic way to—"

"Wait a minute," I said. There had been a considerable delay between the time the phone rang and the time I was told to pick it up. "You didn't tell the astronaut about the dance, did you?"

"No, but what's wrong with telling him? It would make his whole month. He probably thinks you're gay."

I thought about that for a second. *The Astronaut and His Gay Son*—I liked the sound of it. If I could get my hands on some blatantly deviant skin mags, *Bone Homme* or something like that, leave them poorly hidden around the house, I just might earn that disinheritance.

"Let him fret. I'm not sure introducing him to Dub would change his mind, anyway."

"Okay, back to the original question: What are you going to wear?"

"I've got some ideas, nothing definite," I said semi-truthfully. This was Sarah's cue. She instructed me to get a pen and paper and proceeded to tell me exactly what to buy and at which stores.

"Where are all these places?" I asked.

"In the mall . . . where you work . . . where *everything* is in Clear Lake . . . where Grace returns to spawn. . . ."

"Oh." I had only entered Clear Lake Mall through the outdoor access of the Cineplex. "Is this your idea or did Dub tell you to call me? Is she afraid I might show up in a loincloth?"

"What *were* you considering wearing?" Sarah asked, a bit peeved. I scrutinized my Hanes and tweed ensemble in the mirror.

"It doesn't matter. I'll go shopping."

After receiving some final accessorizing tips as well as a mini-dating/etiquette lesson, I clicked the phone's flash button and got a new dial tone. This would be the one part of the morning I would enjoy. After seven rings, Doug answered.

"Stewart Copeland residence," he exhaled into the phone.

I could hear the irregular thwacking of a novice drummer coming from behind him. "Mornin', Sunshine," I intoned. "You hanging a bit?"

"This is not a joke. I will pay you one million dollars to terminate my brother. Let me repeat, just so you don't misunderstand: This *is* solicitation for murder. You will receive payment in small bills, some coins, and pool cleaning equipment when I see the body."

I answered in a Marlon-Brando-as-Godfather-marbles-in-cheeks accent. "I will do this for you, but one day I will ask from you a favor."

I could almost hear him smile. "Tell me everything I did last night. Was I charming? Amusing? Did I puke on anyone?"

"Oh, it was a night of love for we young GODs," I began. "I watched our nicknamed comrades Zipper and Veg play footsie right in front of me. My spurned lady threw herself at wee Matt. Oh, yeah, and I asked Dub to the homecoming dance."

San Diego, Senior Year

I sat at my desk, sorting through the day's bounty of letters from schools entreating recently recognized swami Steven Richard York to grace their "campi." (Had I mentioned my middle name reflects the astronaut's endorsement of a certain president who had resigned?) I separated them according to their proximity to the Pacific Ocean. Any school more than fifty miles away from a beach was tossed. I held on to the Harvard application on a lark.

"Steve?" Sarah tapped on my door.

"Yeah?"

"Can I come in?"

I hadn't received many visitors in my chambers, but I gave my sister permission to enter. Reflexively I scanned the room for drug paraphernalia, soiled underwear, stray condoms. (This was a completely gratuitous search, but I'm sure I'm not the only eighteen-year-old who can't help himself.) Sarah sat on my made bed, her only option save the floor and the chair I was sitting in.

"Mother is insane."

It wasn't a claim I necessarily agreed with, but I thought I should concur. We were in new territory here. Historically, we had only discussed my assorted neuroses.

Sarah had never come to me with her problems. Hell, I never thought she had any. "She has moments of temporary insanity. She usually gets over it."

"I'm going to go see Pearl Jam whether she lets me or not." I didn't believe this for a second. Sarah bent down and began thumbing through my collegiate discard pile. "You're trashing Columbia . . . Cornell . . . ?"

"Anything that begins with *C*," I said quickly.

"Dartmouth?"

"I don't own a winter coat. Have you been to New Hampshire in January?"

"Will you talk to Mom for me?"

"She's pretty pissed—mainly about what you said to Chuck. You were pretty hard on him."

"Remind me to tell you a story about Chuck someday. I don't really care what Chuck thinks is proper. Besides, on the short list of those who shouldn't talk about being hard on people . . ."

I think she was referring to me.

"I'll talk to Mom."

"Thanks, Bro." She walked to the door but turned before leaving. "I'm sorry for dragging you into the battle the other night. You seem like you're doing a lot better lately."

Houston, Sophomore Year

I left home at four o'clock dressed in my ridiculous work uniform, made a show of saying good-bye to the old man still camped in front of the television, then wished I hadn't. My acknowledgment of his presence was an anomaly that I hoped wouldn't give me away. I had sur-reptitiously phoned Dub from my bedroom an hour earlier. Our call had included zero frivolity. Watches were synchronized, plans drawn. No observer would have accused us of flirting. Honestly, I was relieved she remembered we were going out.

I zoomed to Doug's, not out of anxiety, but because I was unable to master the Lincoln's innate horsepower. Grazing the accelerator with my toe created a g force I felt certain was mussing up my exhaustively styled hair. The Lincoln seemed ideal for an important date. Given the vastness of the interior, however, witch doctors sacrificing chickens in the backseat would have gone unnoticed.

I was greeted at the Chappell residence by Doug's good-natured mother, Frieda. She told me Doug was upstairs practicing. I could already hear him drumming, but the way she said "practicing" made it sound like he would be auditioning for the Met the following week. I found Doug on his trap set wearing headphones. On his bedstand I counted four empty packets of Alka-Seltzer. He stopped when he saw me. He put down his sticks and took off his headphones.

"I'll say this for you, Lippy, you go to the dance dressed like that, and you've got more balls than me."

I had to leave my house early to convince the astronaut I was heading to work, but even with a shopping trip to break up the monotony, the five-hour intermission prior to picking up Dub was excruciatingly slow in passing. Doug found a copy of *This Is Spinal Tap* in the debris winning the battle for the closet doorway. He slipped it into the VCR in his room. We both had the dialogue memorized, but my fidgeting and pacing kept us from enjoying it one more time. After my eleventh pilgrimage to the window to check on the Lincoln, Doug paused the movie with the remote control, got off his bed, and staggered into the bathroom he shared with Stan. He motioned me to follow. There he lifted the top off the commode and withdrew a dripping Red Stripe. He held it away from his body with his thumb and index finger, not quite ready, himself, for the hair of the dog.

"Take this and calm down. Be a man."

I drank a pair, and by the time I got dressed, I was sufficiently composed. I had stashed my new dress clothes, all $211 worth, at Doug's place. I needed five attempts to get my $40—Sarah had insisted on silk—tie from obscuring my crotch or exposing my belly à la *Carpet Salesman's Quarterly*, but upon successful completion, I confess to feeling a bit splashy.

"Maybe after the dance, you can do my taxes," Doug said, appraising my new look somewhat more critically. He took a stick of Wrigley's out of a pack on the floor and handed it to me. "Beer breath, a dating *no* when meeting parents."

I checked my watch. It was 8:38, time to go. I returned to the bathroom and rechecked my teeth for gunk, then, nodding to my friend, departed. I arrived at Dub's at 8:56, a decidedly uncool four minutes early. Her house was plantation style with four white wooden pillars supporting a porch that circled the house. The slave quarters, I assumed, were out back. I considered driving around the block for the next ten minutes, but decided that since my Speed Stick was still at full strength, it would behoove me to make my appearance now. I switched off the ignition, put the keys in my pocket, a bit concerned about the lump they made in my slacks, and forced myself to walk deliberately to the door.

I secretly wished a Varner female would answer the door, or better yet, Dub would dash out and say, "Quick, let's make a break for your car before you have to meet my parents." I got neither. A brick of a man I assumed was Dub's father appeared in the doorway.

"You must be Steve," he said, offering me his hand. "Come in. Come in." I had dried my hands on the back of my slacks nonstop from the car to the door, yet I still felt like I was handing the Dub *père* a slice of Spam. He stepped out of the doorframe, revealing his wife. "I'm Francis and this is Maureen."

I moistened Maureen's hand as well. My preconceptions of the couple had been based solely on my "I Never" knowledge of their marijuana dabbling. I realized as I met them that I had expected a VW bus in the driveway, a bearded Francis, and a bell-bottomed Maureen. Instead, Francis was balding, an inch shorter than me and a hundred pounds heavier. Maureen's straight black hair appeared natural, unlike her daughter's. Maureen had the camera. My "likewise pleased to meet you" response sounded like an audition for the Vienna Boys' Choir.

I had envisioned a grand stairway down which Dub would make her entrance. I also assumed she would need to be beckoned, but she appeared from somewhere in the back of the house, saving me from prolonged chitchatting with the adults.

"You look nice," she said, stealing what should have been my opening line.

"So do you," I eeped. Dub's hair was up, held by a magical clip that allowed the excess to cascade in hot iron-curled shoots down the back of her neck. Wisps of bangs had been purposely freed from the clip, and they hung down to Dub's lovely eyebrows. She had obviously coordinated the green vintage dress she wore with her eyes. White gloves covered her arms up to her elbows. The Varners beamed. Maureen pushed us together, stepped back and clicked off a half dozen frames.

From what I understood, the small gym was the perennial home of the homecoming dance while the prom alternated between the parallel lavishness of the Four Seasons and Ritz Carlton. We drove to Grace, making mirthless small talk about how we hoped we'd see Bill and Holly, how outdated and mainstream we imagined the music would be, the fluky nippishness of Clear Lake's early cold season. Dub sat so far away from me that I wasn't able to see her in my peripheral vision when I drove.

As Sarah had instructed, I parked the Lincoln and raced around to the other side to open Dub's door, but the car was so huge I couldn't circumnavigate it in time. She exited the craft unassisted. We joined the procession bound for tropical paradise. At the door Dub opened her purse as if we were going Dutch on the admission. I magnanimously refused her money. The bowels of the darkened gym were, as Holly had described to Lynnette, all construction paper and cheese. We sat across from each other in molded plastic chairs at a long cafeteria table that had been covered gloriously with white butcher paper. It was quickly obvious that we were operating on sophomore time; the football game wasn't even over yet. A half-dozen ten-galloned couples shuffled around the jump ball circle to the yodeling of Garth Brooks. After an hour notable for stretches of staring at the dance floor by Dub, staring at the exit sign by me, separate and extended trips to the rest room, the playing of the love theme from *Beauty and the Beast,* and a deliberation on what our friends were doing that evening, a whooping and delirious throng seemed to instantly take over the gym in an orgy of bloodlust and school spirit. Dub leaned over to me.

"Looks like we kicked a whole bunch of ass tonight."

Dub and I spotted Bill and Holly at the same time. We both stood and waved our arms frantically to get their attention. They acted surprised to see us. They pulled up two chairs on Dub's side of the table and sat close to each other, underscoring the distance between

Dub and me. Holly challenged Bill to join the football players who were slam-dunking some unfortunate girl's mum in a crepe-papered rim. Bill pretended to get up to join the fray, but Holly pulled him back down and kissed his cheek.

The DJ played a five-year-old Peter Gabriel song, and Holly grabbed Bill's hand to pull him on the dance floor. I noticed with some annoyance that he didn't appear nearly reluctant enough. Dub looked imploringly at me.

"I, uh, don't dance," I said, making it sound like I was a member of some cult that forbade it.

"If you don't want to dance, it's fine with me, but do you mind if I dance with Bill and Holly?"

"Yeah. Go ahead." I slouched in my chair and watched as the trio edged out onto the floor. Bill and Holly danced, as did most students there, like speed skaters pushing off their opposite leg with each beat, celebrating each successful stomp with an intermittent clap, whereas Dub created her own dance microcosm. Dub's hands stretched high above her head where they seemed to be kneading an invisible lump of dough. Her feet were stationary, but her knees, hips, and shoulders swung hypnotically. She kept her eyes shut, and her ear rested against one of her upraised shoulders. In her queer dance I grasped, for the first time, the difference between sensuality and some athletic Fly Girl's simulated banging.

When Dub returned to the table, she sat next to me instead of across from me. I couldn't help but think that was a good sign. In the refracted squares of light supplied by the tropical paradise mirror ball, I could see Dub glistening, looking happier. Cassandra Holbrook seized the mike and interrupted a Madonna song to announce importantly that the coronation ceremony was about to begin. Now, ordinarily, this would have been a proclamation either Dub or I would have mocked ("Ooh, should we move closer?" "God! I can't watch!"), but in the presence of two nominees who happened to be our friends, we kept our sarcasm internal.

Within fifteen minutes Bill and Holly were sitting back next to us, looking no worse for their loss to a toothy Buc Babe and cement-truck-looking fullback. Missy had been right about the time most people spent at the dance. After the royalty ceremony, people who came in an hour after us were already splitting. The DJ, not oblivious of the exodus, shifted into his one-to-one, then two-to-one, slow-song-to-fast-song ratio. Slow dancing interested me. There didn't seem to be much to it. Partners locked themselves into a first-round wrestling clinch and spun, taking thirty to forty-five seconds to complete a rotation. I tried watching feet, looking for some mystery step that would reveal me as a slow dancing impostor if I were to get out on the floor. I saw none. Though our tension had eased with the camaraderie and Dub's foray onto the dance floor, the two of us still weren't saying much. When I saw her mouthing the words to "With or Without You," I worked up my nerve.

"Would you like to dance?" *Dance* seemed like a funny word. No one was dancing—they were mauling and groping. In essence, I had just asked Dub if she wouldn't mind following me out to the middle of a crowded room where I would proceed to affix myself to her. I wish I could have managed something cooler, a "Care to join me?" with my crooked elbow accepting only yes as an answer.

"Sure," she said, and she took my hand, palm to palm, and led me out onto the floor of the gym.

I can't say I remember much about the rest of the U2 song. I was too concerned with sliding my feet and putting my hands in the proper lower back loci. I watched other couples rather than Dub, factoring their rotation, sway, body separation, and tried to adjust my own accordingly. When the song ended, I relaxed, congratulated myself for going undetected, and headed for base— our table. But Dub held me firm, and as one of those drearier English bands equated love and death, she took over leading duties. First, she closed the distance between us. Then, using her hands, she positioned my head so that I was looking at her. She squeezed me and rocked us in time to the music. I hadn't realized before that slow songs had a beat. I became aware of Dub, her smell, the way she felt, her breath on my neck. I know it's a cliché, but I really did notice the curve of her back. For the first time since asking her to the dance, I was happy I had. All that time in geometry, wishing I were with her, wishing I were touching her, and here I was. I had been a rap song away from completely missing the experience.

We returned to our table holding hands (fingers interlocked). Dub had taken my hand, but I think I might have made the move had she not. Neither of us let go when we sat down.

"I am very happy right now," I said like a dork.

"You're not thinking of getting us a room, are you?" Dub said, eyes widening in facetious anticipation.

"Already booked. And tell me now if you're not planning on putting out, because I know plenty of women who will."

"Probably all friends of mine," she said, winning the exchange. We grinned, and for the first time since Holly and Bill joined us, we were oblivious to them.

San Diego, Senior Year

Matching blue envelopes lay on the bar that divided the kitchen from the family room when I got home from Cap's today. One was addressed to Sarah, the other to me. I knew they were from the astronaut without reading the name. How many other people use an American flag icon on their return mail stickers? Given the dimensions and sameness of the envelopes, I guessed them to be invitations of some sort.

I nuked a hot dog and tortilla. I ate at the counter without disturbing the letter.

•••

The next day—for the second time in less than a week—Sarah came into my bedroom. It was starting to feel like a Who concert in here. In her right hand was the blue envelope I had ignored the previous day. The left hand clutched her letter, already ripped open.

"Read it," she ordered.

"What is it? Let me guess. He wants us to show up dressed like a gentleman and young lady to the Space Travelers Logrolling Convention? Houston Bigwig Elbow-Rubbing Seminar? Senator Ass-Kissing Competition?"

Sarah didn't think I was funny. "Just open it."

I slid my index finger under the envelope flap and carefully peeled it open. I found, as expected, an invitation inside.

I'll be damned. The astronaut's getting married.

Houston, Sophomore Year

Dub sat in the same area code with me in the Lincoln front seat on the way home. Trey had stopped by our table and invited the four of us to a party at the Ritz Carlton that a bunch of his jock friends were having. What a guy! I couldn't accept, though, because I had to arrive home before 1 A.M.—my standard home-from-work time, lest the astronaut get suspicious about the

Lincoln. Dub was going through the old man's somewhat limited tape collection.

"Put in the Goo Goo Dolls," I said, aware of the actual selection.

"No Goo Goo Dolls. But can I interest you in *Hank Williams's Greatest Hits, Improving Your Putting with Ben Crenshaw,* or some tape with the all the letters worn off?"

"Put that one in." I knew it to be Neil Diamond's *Hot August Night.* When we were kids, Sarah and I used to beg the astronaut to play it on long trips. Of course, I wasn't about to admit this to Dub.

"I don't know," Dub said, weighing the tapes in her hands. "My putting completely sucks."

She put the Neil Diamond cassette in, nevertheless. Lush sounds of Spanish guitars and violins glided out of the speakers.

Right mood/wrong generation. If I were taking a middle-aged woman home, I'd have to pull the car over right now to be ravaged. My future with Dub was less certain. My stomach threatened to convulse with each block nearer we drew to her front door.

As I docked the Lincoln in the Varner driveway I checked the windows of the house to see which had lights still on: two upstairs . . . downstairs was dark save the porch light. This time I managed to make it around the car in time to open the door for Dub. As she got out, I stupidly put my hands in my pockets. She took hold of my biceps anyway. I tried to flex very slowly, so she wouldn't notice me doing it. When we made it to the door, she spoke.

"Thanks for taking me to the dance. I know I've been kind of a bitch all week. You didn't deserve that. It's just sort of a girl solidarity thing."

I wanted to say, "You're right. And now that you're

my woman, don't let it happen again or I may just cut you loose." But what I said was, "It was my fault."

"No, it wasn't. It wasn't your fault, and if you want to know the truth, I wasn't acting that way because I was sticking up for Rhonda. I think I was just being jealous."

"Really?"

After I said it, she just looked at me. Three or four seconds maybe. She was savoring the moment. I don't think it mattered to her one way or the other whether I tried to kiss her. She was a scientist measuring my response. She smiled as she reached up for the front door handle. I'm not sure where I found the nerve, but I grabbed her hand. We quickly weaved our fingers together. I reached out for her shoulder with my other hand and leaned in toward her mouth. Her empty left hand came in under my arm and intercepted my head. At first I thought she was going to stop me. Instead, she held my chin softly and guided me toward her lips. I had snuck quick lip licks on the walk to the porch, but I was afraid her staredown had allowed them to dry and crack. It didn't matter; hers were wet enough for both of us. She kissed me softly. Slowly she moved from my lower to upper lip. Her hand let go of my chin. She brought it up to the back of my neck, running her fingers through my hair and leaving her thumb on my ear. Then she backed away. She looked at me and tried to stifle a laugh. I think I was smiling pretty big.

San Diego, Senior Year

Though an electric fan rotated methodically and a lone window was open as far as the crank-controlled school sort allow, the stench left no doubt that someone had puked in DeMouy's office. The buzz of the fluorescent lighting punc-

tuated the fact that DeMouy wasn't, for the first time since I
had been sent to him, jamming to the sounds of Mother
Nature. The man himself looked disconsolate. Slouched in
his chair, DeMouy rested his cheek against the back of his
overlapping hands, which in turn covered a disorganized pile
of memos and forms on the desk. The counselor had lost his
trademark crispness. The routine Japanese precision of his
hair part had given way to a three-day-hike-in-a-stocking cap
matting. A line of blood was beading up across the visible side
of his neck. His creased tie hung from his desk lamp, and
black coffee replaced herbal tea in his Far Side mug.

"Rough day?" I asked.

I could see DeMouy focusing on me. I decided I should
try to help.

"DeMouy," I queried, "did you have a happy childhood?
Do you remember not getting something you always wanted
for Christmas and really hating your parents because of it?
Was going into education a way to get even with them?"

"I sent for you yesterday," he answered coldly.

I thought about returning when he was in a better
mood. Whatever he needed me for could wait. I finished
scanning the office: trash basket on its side, fern branches
broken, mop bucket filled with detergent-blue water.

"Did I miss a fight?"

DeMouy nodded.

"And somebody puked?"

He nodded again. He raised his torso, and I saw that
his button-down featured a wet spot roughly the size and
shape of Connecticut. He began halfheartedly sorting
through the papers on his desk.

"You've never had to break up a fight before, have
you?"

DeMouy found the college info he had been searching for and handed it across his desk to me.

"I'm thirty today," he said.

"Kids," I said, shaking my head.

Houston, Sophomore Year

The next day Dub and I decided to drive down to Galveston. I dressed in attire more befitting nonconformist convention—muskrat-holed blue jeans graffitied with lyrics to my favorite songs, Screaming Trees T-shirt, oversized lumberjack-thick flannel overshirt, dragonfly fishing lure earring (used to catch porpoises and eels). We lunched at Captain Pegleg's on a deck that overlooked the typically wimpish Gulf noted for its eighteen-inch-high waves breaking ten feet from the shore, packed brown sand, and detergent green water. We were the only two who chose to eat outside in the cold, and our middle-aged waitress seemed unimpressed by our stoicism. Afterward I took Dub to see a movie. I made a couple of disparaging remarks about the projectionist's obliviousness of a focus problem before inching a tentative pinkie over to Dub's hand. We shared a bucket of popcorn and a large Pepsi. We drank from the same straw.

It wasn't difficult to find a deserted stretch of beach where we could park. Dub didn't ask where we were heading, and I didn't volunteer any information. I had a kite wedged behind her seat that I would use as Plan B if Dub started freaking about my tender notions. My timing was perfect, though. I pointed my car toward the ocean in time to catch the last few minutes of the sunset. I pushed in the *Best of Bread* eight track that I had cued up to "Everything I Own."

"*Rico suave,*" Dub responded.

We watched the sunset through her passenger-side window. I delighted in the back of Dub's head. She turned to say something, but I reached over and kissed her. We kissed with the gentleness of the previous evening, but Dub started making noises low in her throat and was soon licking my teeth and biting my lips. I made my first tentative probes of the inside of her mouth. My left arm was supporting all my weight, though, and it began to shudder. I leaned back and pulled Dub across my lap. We made out furiously. I didn't even worry that she might notice my car wasn't a standard.

San Diego, Senior Year

The curved, carpeted walls of Mom's cubicle provided nearly 270 degrees of wasted bulletin board potential. I was tempted to make use of it for her. I don't know how she gets anything accomplished with all the crap strewn across the top of her desk. I swear, she's messier than Sarah. Manila folders and faxes covered most of the work space and buried the nameplate declaring this the domain of CINDY BLACK, REAL ESTATE AGENT. The only items she had tacked up were citations as top seller for the last two quarters and photos—one each of Chuck, Sarah, and me. The shot of me had been taken the summer after my freshman year. I stood beside my supervisor, Mr. Lozano. We had posed, unintentionally, like farmer and wife in *American Gothic*. I held my rake in the same determined manner as my precursor gripped his pitchfork. Even then I was taller than my boss, though my chest was concave and I could have played Peter Pan in just about anyone's cast. I wondered if she chose this particular photo because it recalled the prepsycho, dopefiend days of Steve.

When I first visited Mom here more than three years ago, I couldn't see over the cubicle walls. Now I rested my chin on top of one and waited for her to get off the phone.

"Well, hello," she said, replacing the phone on its hook. "It's been a long time since you've been down to the office."

"I was thinking of getting a place. You know, striking out on my own."

"Ah, and what price range were you looking at?"

"Oh, something in the ten-twelve range,"

"Mil?"

"No, dollars. Ten to twelve dollars."

"We're going to have a tough time finding something with a pool in that bracket. A young, single man like yourself probably wants a pool."

"What the hell. I'll go fifteen. Man, you're good."

"Yes, I am," my mother said. "So what really brings you down here?"

"Sarah," I said. "She asked me to talk to you about the Pearl Jam concert." Mom crossed her legs and folded her arms across her chest. "Okay, here goes." I had rehearsed most of this on my way to Mom's office. "I know all the people Sarah's going with. Well, not really know them, but know who they are. They're a regular who's who at school—all good kids, teacher's wet dreams, straight arrows. And Sarah . . . jeez, you know as well as I do she'd be a *total* bust as a rock and roll degenerate. She's too careful and level-headed. I mean, she might sign a pact with the devil, but she'd check him out with *Consumer Reports,* just to make sure his customers were getting good value for their souls.

"Besides, most of these people are just friends. They're not looking at this as a romantic getaway. And even if they were, what could they do in a hotel room with six other people?"

Mom unfolded her arms and began tapping the eraser tip of her pencil on a mound of forms. "And what about the drinking?"

"Everyone drinks. At least Sarah is abnormally responsible. I don't think she would get in a car with anyone who was fu— messed up."

"Are you planning to go to your father's wedding?"

This certainly came from left field.

"I haven't thought much about it. When is it? I didn't read the invitation very carefully." I knew the wedding would be in Houston, a town in which I had sworn never to set foot again.

"The beginning of August."

"I don't think so."

"It would kill your father if you didn't show up for the wedding."

"I doubt it. He didn't even call to ask us."

"He was probably afraid to talk to you, afraid the two of you would fight. Communication never was his strong suit, or yours for that matter. But I know him—he needs you and Sarah there. Sarah will go, but I'm not so sure about you. I can't make you go."

"There's more to it than just that. . . ."

Mom leaned toward me and took my forearms, just like she had Sarah's outside that Broadway theater years ago.

"I know, honey. I know."

Houston, Sophomore Year

You know in movies how they speed through the sickening falling-in-love thing by showing clips of the couple walking along the beach holding hands, studying together until one of the wiseacres tosses a pillow at the other, riding a two-seated bicycle in the rain? Feel free to insert said footage now, though I don't think we did any of that, and I'm positive in regard to the two-seated bicycle. My recollection is we made out a lot and talked on the phone.

I conceded York Manor entirely to the astronaut and began spending all my time at the Varners'. Francis ran his own advertising firm called Solutions! and Maureen was an editor for *Texas Monthly,* but they both arranged ways to make it home for dinner. Francis cooked—pasta for the most part—and the women of the house cleaned. None of them, he claimed, could boil water. Neither Wanda, Maureen, nor Dub's older sister, Sylvia, took offense at his assertion. The ironic aspect, I always thought, was that given the first names of the Varner women, they really should have opened a diner. (Dub explained to me sometime later that she and her sister had both been named for famed great-great aunts, key players in the suffrage movement.) The novelty of parents younger than forty never lost its power to astonish me. Francis blasted his complete Rolling Stones CD collection over a state-of-the-art Yamaha stereo system. This despite Dub's and my phony studying at the dining room table aimed at disguising the serious footsy action below. I could see him in the kitchen air-guitaring "Can't You Hear Me Knockin.' " It took several scoldings from the Varner elders before I would refer to them by their first names.

At school, anyone who cared could have recognized that the two of us were a couple. We walked each other to class. We went to lunch together. We shared our lockers. But, please, we weren't one of those couples attempting conception against the classroom doors, stretching salivary umbilical cords every time they parted.

"So when am I going to meet your little girlfriend?"

The astronaut smirked at me. If there had been any doubt in his mind when he asked the question whether I did, in fact, have a girlfriend, my hand-in-the-cookie-jar reaction erased it. In the three weeks I had been seeing Dub, neither she nor I had called the other girl/boyfriend. I admit I liked her being referred to by that title.

"She's not my girlfriend. She's just a friend," I lied. I screwed the lid back on the jar of mayonnaise we had been sharing.

"Well, you're sure spending a lot of time with her," he said, sealing the Baggie of sliced turkey. "I think it's great that you're starting to take an interest in girls."

Like I had just noticed them.

The astronaut was in his pajamas (tops and bottoms). He had come back downstairs for a midnight snack at the same time I was returning from a night at the Cineplex. I was surprised he had been able to deduce anything about my personal life. I had always assumed that Mom briefed him about his children's affairs while he listened absently and requested more coffee over the morning sports page.

"I'd like to meet her. Even if she is only a friend."

Why? I thought. *So you could disapprove of her, too?* But I said nothing. I filled my mouth with sandwich and gave a noncommittal grunt.

San Diego, Senior Year

The bullfrog-deep voice, the clipped and precise diction, left no doubt about the identity of the caller. My only previous conversation with the astronaut came long distance at Christmas. He spent his holiday at his soon-to-be in-laws' in North Carolina; I spent mine in San Diego. He called to thank Sarah for the monogrammed, leather racquetball gym bag and me for the shirt (Sarah picked it out; I paid for it). I thanked him for the shirt (a bronze, polished cotton Perry Ellis with jade buttons, the stylishness of which left no doubt his fiancée had picked it out).

This time he called expressly to talk to me.

"Steve, congratulations. I just heard."

"About what?"

"About being named a Merit finalist. That's very impressive."

Where was he going with this? I took note of his phrasing: "very impressive," not "great" or "I'm proud of you." Nope, his concern was with how other people would view the accomplishment.

"I just got lucky," I said.

"Nonsense, you've got great blood. Your mother is a very smart lady." He chuckled, but I heard something in his voice, something unfamiliar. If I didn't know better, I'd swear it was uneasiness—a condition on which I thought I had the York monopoly. He continued, "So where are you thinking of going to school?"

"Dunno."

He didn't speak immediately. I figured he was contemplating how hard he could push me about the right college or whether he should shoot for a reverse psychology approach and conspicuously avoid the subject. When he eventually spoke, I understood it was neither.

"Steve, I have a favor to ask."

I didn't respond.

"I was hoping you would be the best man at my wedding."

Certainly not, I wanted to say. *What makes you think I would? Is your life really so pathetic that you'd feel compelled to ask me? Isn't there some other fastidious, fascist, jet jockey who'd consider it an honor to be in an American hero's wedding? God, don't you have any friends?* Deeply perturbed and disoriented by this conversation, I gazed out the sliding glass doors leading to the back porch, wishing I could escape through them. Beyond was the Pacific, a vast gray-green slate crawling with bright reflections from the low hanging sun. The orange glow of the horizon reminded me of my second date with Dub, a kite lodged behind my backseat . . . just in case. I felt tears sneaking in behind my eyes.

"I'll probably have college orientation around that time," I said. It was a lame excuse: Most colleges run orientations all summer.

"It's a standing invitation," the astronaut said. "Let me know . . . when you know something for sure." Again I thought I heard anxiety in his voice, but I didn't have time to consider the ramifications—I was about to lose it.

"All right," I said. I hung up immediately. I ran up to my room and pulled the Battleship game down from the shelf in my closet.

Houston, Sophomore Year

My girlfriend spoon-fed me another bite of Banana Pudding Blizzard as I lay across her lap in the El Camino in the Dairy Queen parking lot. We had become an official couple—licensed to use the terms *boyfriend* and *girlfriend*—a week earlier. Our geometry teacher, Mrs. Lanigan, had called us down for the second time, not very aggressively—we were both acing her class—but she croaked something about hating having couples in her class. This elicited an obligatory *ooooh* chorus. Exiting the classroom, Dub assured Mrs. Lanigan that she would try to keep her "boyfriend" in line. After that, we quit correcting acquaintances who spoke of us in those terms. The two of us never discussed it.

"Why don't you get along with your father?" Dub asked, shoveling another bite in my mouth. The ice cream gave me time to frame my answer eruditely.

"He's a dick."

"Thank you for that contemplative and comprehensive assessment." She tapped my nose with the dripping plastic spoon.

"What do you want to know?"

"He must have done something to you; you hate him so much."

I sat up and faced her. "I can't stand the fact he's in better shape than me. I hate it that he buys American. He watches CNN nonstop. He drinks bottled water. He reads the entire newspaper, section by section, and he folds it back the way it was delivered. He thinks it's normal to work sixteen hours a day. He's never air-guitared the Rolling Stones. Hell, I don't think he knows who they are."

"Well, I can see what you mean. I don't see how you put up with it."

"Okay, those are just the things that piss me off on a day-to-day basis. You want to know what really gets me?" She nodded. "I always feel like I'm disappointing him, like he's waiting for his share of the gene pool to kick in. I'm sure he thinks that one day I'm going to rush into a burning building and save an orphan's life or jump out of the stands at a football game and run back a punt for the winning touchdown, and then he'll finally know, 'Yep, that's my boy.' "

"Would you even tell him if you saved an orphan?"

"Hell, no. I'd lose my only weapon against him . . . if he were proud of me." The conversation was becoming increasingly uncomfortable for me. I sat up and put my key in the ignition.

"So why do you need a weapon?"

"Because of what he did to Mom."

"Which is . . . ?"

"He stole from her. Years of her life she can never get back. He treated her like a show pony who did the dishes. I'm just happy that she finally got rid of him, and you know what? I don't think the astronaut even saw it coming."

"Sarah doesn't seem to have a problem with him. *She* even calls him Dad."

"Sarah's a couple years younger than me. She doesn't remember everything as clearly as I do." I turned up the stereo and drove us back to school.

San Diego, Senior Year

"Yo, Bro!"

The Wakefield hallways were jammed and I couldn't see Sarah, but I knew she was out there somewhere. I spotted her on the third step of the stairs leading to the foreign language classrooms. She beckoned me like an over-animated traffic cop—the kind you see only in television commercials.

"You are a stud!" she said when I got near enough.

"Yes . . . and?" I did the rotating-backward handflip, implying more information should follow.

"Mom said I could go to the Pearl Jam concert."

"Bonus," I said, mimicking my idiot stoner friends.

"Yeah, whatever line you fed her, she swallowed it. But what really sold her was when I told her you'd be going with us." Sarah fished two tickets out of her book bag and pressed them into my hand. "You owe me fifty bucks."

Houston, Sophomore Year

I stopped tracing the letters that spell *I want you now* on Dub's back when I heard the announcement.

"Trumpet a new age! Desecrate rosemary and sage! Frail as puppy love! New and improved dadaists, Pizza Hut beckons. Thursday six P.M. Be there or be a polygon."

Dub swiveled. "Did you know anything about a meeting?"

"No." I was still considering the possible intentions of that *frail-as-puppy-love* business. Okay, so I'll admit that maybe I wasn't spending much time with Doug. Maybe I had let a couple messages slip by without returning his calls, but I had a girlfriend now. He needed to grow up, get it through his head.

I had every intention of querying Doug, not only about his word choice, but his failure to notify me—his appointed public relations specialist—about a meeting. I didn't get a chance to ask, however, before the next evening at the Hut. I picked up Dub from her house, but we were running late and the meeting had been called to order before we arrived. Doug neither paused nor looked at us as we took the available seats in the back of the room.

"The talent show is right after lunch the Friday before Christmas break. People with tickets can skip sixth period and go home when the show's over, so you know everybody's going to be there. I thought we could come up with something to shock the sheep."

"Wanda," Doug said, using my girlfriend's Christian name, "you're usually good for an idea. Any inspired suggestions?"

"Momentarily," Dub answered saltily. She let go of my hand.

"How about something multimedia. Something like

you did with the video camera," Veg said.

Several members nodded. Trey suggested we keep brainstorming, and the onslaught began. Everyone, save Trey and me, had a vision. I made faces at the especially batty suggestions; he jotted everything down, regardless. It wasn't until the arrival of the food that the floor came open again. Bill spoke.

"Trey, which of the ideas do you think we should do?"

Trey looked around the table. "I think we should do all of them."

San Diego, Senior Year

I felt sorry for Jeff DeMouy. As he continued to tap a humming microphone, the some three hundred seniors assembled before him volleyed gargantuan wads of paper—the handouts DeMouy had prepared for the session—like spectators given beach balls at Padres games.

"All right, everybody, listen up."

Few students stopped their conversations or diverted their attention from their paper-wad games.

"You're not going to lunch until we're done here!"

This time people shut up. DeMouy used the silence to speak of graduation. The materials in our hands, he said—or in some cases, the materials that had been compacted—contained information about graduation gowns and mortarboards, how many people we could invite to the ceremony, class rings, invitations, and order forms for the yearbook. DeMouy pointed to tables set up around the gym where we could carry out the tasks set forth in the paperwork.

"If graduation is still in doubt for you, we've highlighted your name on your report card. And one last thing, you can get your prom bids at the table by the drinking fountain." DeMouy stepped away from the podium. The crowd booed him again. This time just for the warm, robust feeling of esprit de corps it provided.

I walked over to the table where report cards were being distributed. There I was surprised to discover I was making a couple A's. It had been a long time since I had seen a report card that wasn't completely consonants. The only comment appearing on my report card was a "showing improvement" from my anatomy teacher, Mr. Reyes, who had awarded me a C nonetheless. Due to the missing English credit, my name was highlighted in yellow. I scanned the gym for a line that didn't seem overwhelming. I spotted Allison Kimble joining the back of the graduation-gown-measuring column. I moseyed up beside her.

Allison wasn't difficult to pick out of the Wakefield crowd. While other girls fell in with the low-maintenance Marcia Brady trend—long, straight, center-parted hair, poufy, midriff-baring tops, bell-bottom jeans with ragged hems, and cork-soled clogs—Allison was significantly behind, or ahead of, the times, depending on how you view fashion cycles. Her brown hair was pulled back and French-braided into a thick, shoulder-length ponytail. Today she wore a red-and-green tartan skirt with a knee-length hem, a plain, starched white blouse, white ankle socks, and tan-and-white oxfords. She looked like a schoolgirl in an AC/DC video—*before* the innocent hears Angus play. She didn't see me approach because she was, as usual, scanning her organizer/planner.

"Check Saturday. See if you're busy that night." Allison faced me and opened her mouth, but nothing came out. She turned her attention back to her planner and began flipping pages. My palms stayed dry. My heart padded along lackadaisically.

"It looks like I've got that night open," Allison said. Then she appraised me suspiciously. "But I'm sure I could think of something. Why?"

I was wearing my Cap's T-shirt—the one with their slogan, BEAN THERE, DONE CAP'S. I mention this only because I became conscious of how odd the two of us would look on a date together. Most of my cohorts were still covering their T-shirts with high-priced grunge flannels bought in malls at Urban Wearfair. Flannel in a San Diego spring. Shoot me if I ever do this.

"I've got tickets to Pearl Jam. Do you want to go?"

"Sounds great," she said.

There was neither hemming nor hawing. The two of us continued standing in line together. I explained the part about not wanting to drive home after the show. She didn't freak out. We talked about who we would pay the most or travel the farthest to see in concert. I said Soul Asylum. She said Bryan Adams.

So what.

Houston, Sophomore Year

GOD's slot in the talent show put us on after two real crowd pleasers. First was the show choir's choreographed rendition of "We Go Together" from *Grease*. Guess what. The girls wore poodle skirts and ponytails; the boys wore leather jackets and greased their hair back. Some of them, the geekiest by the light of day, even tucked decks of cards inside rolled up T-shirt sleeves to look like cigarette packs. Duh. The senior football players used balloons and wigs to affect sex changes, then danced to "You Are So Beautiful" wearing ballerinas' tights and tutus. The "girls" executed their jetés and pas de quatres as wretchedly as one might imagine, and the sheep bleated with delight at the spectacle. I was busy setting up for my mission from GOD, but I glanced up at the performance to see a 280-pound lineman Baryshnikoving right off the stage and into the crowd. Now *that* was funny.

The crowd grew restless during the lengthy intermission our technical requirements demanded. We walled the back of the stage with three vast screens. Dub and I worked slide projectors aimed at the two outside screens. The middle one was reserved for the Super 8 movie Veg and Doug had filmed for the cause. Those two, along with Bill, had also formed a three-piece band to perform center stage. They had, during their first week of existence, named themselves Get A Grip, but thinking the name too teenish, shortened it to The Grippe, in honor of the disease. Veg learned to play bass in ten days. Doug asked me, originally, if I wanted the position, but I assured him I would be happier offstage, billy-clubbing ten-year-old autograph hounds and auditioning groupies. Besides, I really didn't have time to practice and all that. "Yeah, that hectic schedule of yours. I know what you mean," he said in response. I just blew his sarcasm off.

Setting up our microdada parade was even a bigger pain in the ass than getting the band onstage. We had twined ten red Radio Flyer wagons together. These were to be pulled from stage left to stage right to show off the artwork created by our other members. This artwork had been created in isolation by individual GOD members. There was no unifying theme, and this was the first time any of us would see what the others had done. Unless we operated in some unexplainable synchronicity, this would be a sublime three-minute dadafest. When

Matt dimmed the house lights and the curtains parted, I fired up my projector.

An hour later I was in the principal's office.

I had never been to the principal's office before. Well, maybe once to pick up honor roll citations, but never to face disciplinary measures. At least I had company. I waited with thirteen members of GOD for our fate to be decided.

Though bizarre, our performance had been, for the most part, innocuous. My slide show consisted of tiny plastic World War II miniatures that I had positioned in sundry square dancing routines—thirty Pattons and Rommels do-si-doing to "Turkey in the Straw." Dub had traveled, unbeknownst to me, into the Fifth Ward to get documentary-quality photographs of junkies and hookers. These she interspersed with shots she took of Betty Crocker chocolate cake mixes. The Grippe butchered the Clash's "I'm So Bored with the U.S.A." Our remaining members were responsible for the dada parade: *Skeleton at Typewriter* by Beverly; *Vacuum Cleaner with Handcuffs* by Holly and Samantha; an open, upright coffin occupied by a radiant, white-gowned bride courtesy of Virginia and Zipper; an ornately framed charcoal of a smiley face by Missy and Rhonda; and our grand finale— Trey's basketball backboard and goal featuring an earth globe electrically lit from within and poised for descent through the hoop. Matt added an appropriate touch by lighting the stage with the mirrored disco ball used so effectively at the homecoming dance.

None of that got us in trouble.

It was Veg and Doug's cinematic efforts that had us sweating it out. The two had infused clips of a particularly spirited Grace pep rally with late 1930s footage of a German throng frothily responding to Adolf Hitler. Shots alternated between stone-faced paratroopers and stone-faced linebackers, *sieg-heiling* Berliners and pom-pom thrusting cheerleaders, uniquely mustached führer spitting and uniquely muttonchopped Coach Yeager barking. For the coup de grâce, the two showed a series of wide shots of Clear Lake Mall. The last one, a post-card-worthy clip of the sun setting beyond the mall's rusty spires, they cut off with the mushroom cloud of a nuclear explosion.

The crowd sat silent for a moment as the curtains were drawn. Then someone booed. And someone screamed. I think I may have even heard crying. Within seconds, the rest of the audience found their voices, and the hall began to rock with furious booing and the chant, "GOD sucks! GOD sucks! GOD sucks!"

As we waited for Principal B. J. Stokes to arrive, Doug began opening drawers of the man's desk. He pulled out a cigar, stuffed it in his mouth, and imitated our principal's drawl.

"Prahd. Prahd in yo'sef. Prahd in yo school," he bellowed.

I thought Matt was going to faint. "Stop that. You're gonna get us all kicked out," he said, trembling.

Doug stuffed the cigar in his pocket and returned to our side of the desk. Seconds later, the real McCoy entered and took the seat Doug had just relinquished. When he began speaking, it was impossible not to think of Doug's impression.

"Trey . . . Bill . . ." Stokes said, naming only the senior boys sitting in front of him, "I simply can't believe you were a part of this." He held on to the lapels of his pow-der blue sports coat with fat little fists. "What was it sup-posed to mean, anyway? Did someone think this little film would be funny?"

"It wasn't supposed to mean anything, sir," Trey

answered. "It was dadaistic expression. Totally disconnected, random images meant to make us think about art in a new way."

This didn't register with Stokes. "Son, you showed the mall getting blown up."

"Sir, we'll just be on our way," Doug interjected. "I'm sure you'll want to have a word with those transvestites who were dancing up on the stage before us."

Stokes tightened his grip on his lapels and gritted his teeth. "Don't get cute with me, boy! This is serious. You kids just about started a damned riot in there. It seems your fellow students don't cotton to watching themselves get compared to Nazis up on the big screen." Stokes rose from his chair and assumed a one-cheek perch on the side of his desk next to Trey. "You're right in the middle of a play-off race, son. Don't you have more important things to do with your time?"

This time Bill spoke. "Trey just organized things. He didn't actually shoot the movie. He didn't even know what was in it."

Stokes turned his attention to Bill. "And you. I can recollect you playing 'Jimmy Crack Corn' at Boy Scout camp. What was that crap you were playing up onstage? This Satan-smack-big-dumb-sex shit you kids watch on *Headbangers Ball*—someone explain it to me. I don't get it."

He then turned his gaze on the rest of us, mentally opening our respective discipline files. "I think what you fellas—and ladies—need is a little adult supervision. This club is hereby dissolved. Y'all can't participate in any school events until you find a faculty sponsor.

"Good luck, children," he said as he shooed us out the door.

San Diego, Senior Year

When he came to pick us up for the Pearl Jam concert, I realized why Sarah had kept Danny Rossow hidden prior to date night. He looked worse than I ever had. Where to begin? Ah, yes. He was a skinhead. He was huge—six-three, maybe six-four. His blue jean jacket must have been dragged the length of the Baja 500. The jacket covered a Dr. Dre T-shirt. A chain ran from his belt loop to his wallet. He sported a small opal in his pierced right nostril. He was as square-jawed as Sergeant Rock; no amount of shaving would have eliminated his five o'clock shadow. Though a junior like Sarah, he could have easily gotten away with patting me on the head and telling me to go outside and play. I vaguely remembered seeing him in the halls at school and being frightened. Currently, he was standing underneath a Peña print in our Southwestern-motifed living room, trying to make small talk with my mother.

"So, Danny, how is work down at the radio station?" Mom asked. Danny was such an inappropriate name for this creature. His friends (or victims) surely referred to him as Gor or Herk.

"They're cutting back on interns. Apparently we're taking up too many parking spaces, because we're certainly not a budget concern. I'll find out next week if I still have a job. I'm one of the newest, but they keep telling me I'm doing a great job, so we'll see how it goes." He sounded polite—pedantic even.

Sarah looked uneasy; she suggested we get a move on. Our foursome, Danny, Sarah, Mom, and I, moved as a group toward the door. As we exited, Mom snapped me back in by my wrist.

"You keep an eye out for your sister. Remember she's only sixteen."

"You're wiggin', Cindy. He seemed all right. You could have gotten an Eddie Haskell—someone who compliments your furniture and sullies your daughter." Only lately had I seen Mom in this protective mode. Of course, I hadn't been around for much of Sarah's dating history.

"Remember, you talked me into this."

"Chill pill for Cindy?"

She punched me in the stomach, hard, but I saw it coming. We laughed. "You have a good time, too, boy."

I rolled my eyes and headed out to join my sister and her date. I climbed in the back of Danny's parents' custom van, relieved Mom hadn't gotten a look at this rolling cathouse. Sarah asked me what Mom had said to me in private.

"She told me that Eddie Vedder was tolerable, but he was no Bono."

Danny chuckled; Sarah sneered.

"So, Sis, is this our first-ever double date?"

"And last."

I had planned on taking out my earrings when picking up Allison, but if Danny had the balls to pick up my sister with a rock pinned in his nose, by God, I could wear a couple hoops in my ears. I gave Danny the Taco Bell napkin with the map Allison had drawn to her house.

"Ugh," Danny said, looking at the map. Then he whistled between his teeth.

"What's up?"

"Toto, I don't think we're in Kansas anymore," the San Diego native said. The ominousness of the brawny skinhead delivering this line was not lost on me. Stoplight by stoplight we traveled deeper into urban blightdom. Allison's house, when we found it, was at one time pink and stucco; now it was just stucco with flakes of pink making a futile effort at clinging to the dilapidated façade. The front lawn was small but recently mowed and trimmed. A small cracked sidewalk led to the front door. An all-night convenience store sat kitty-corner to Allison's, and outside it, two vagrants debated the ownership of a cardboard box. I could hear police sirens in two directions.

"Are you sure she wasn't putting you on, man?" Danny asked.

I just hopped out of the van. The thought had occurred to me as well. She dressed, after all, like she had just stepped out of a *Town & Country* ad. I knocked on the flimsy warped plywood of the hollow front door. The action hardly created a sound, but I feared putting my hand through the door if I knocked any harder.

"Coming," I heard from inside. I recognized the voice as Allison's. When she opened the door I caught a glimpse of a bearded man in a terry cloth bathrobe staring blankly at what I had to assume was a television. Allison slipped through the opening and quickly pulled the door shut behind her. "Ready?" she said.

"Yeah."

I introduced Allison to Danny and Sarah. It turned out that Allison and Sarah had been in a required gym class together. They giggled, reminiscing about a square dance unit their instructor had introduced.

"Square dancing," Sarah said, "has anything ever been named so perfectly?"

Allison wore a green mock turtleneck and a Gap vest. It wasn't quite the Viper Room, but it wasn't *The 700 Club* either. Allison and I occupied the two captain's chairs immediately behind Danny and Sarah. We picked up the remaining half of our eightsome at the home of Sarah's best friend, Lindsay Thompson. They crammed themselves on the bench seat in the back of the van, and we left San Diego on the two-hour drive to the Forum.

●●●

In my dream, I was graduating from Grace High School. The ceremony was taking place in the Astrodome, but someone had forgotten to turn on the air-conditioning. My blue gown had gone purple in the pools of sweat on my chest and arms. Beads of sweat from my forehead dripped down and into my eyes. Dub sat next to me, oblivious to the heat and my hand gripping hers. No matter how hard I squeezed her hand, I couldn't get her to face me. I dug my fingernails into the back of her hand, creating bloody quarter moons—still nothing. I screamed her name, but she didn't hear me. No one did. The procession of graduates continued across the stage.

I woke with Allison's hair in my mouth. We were sharing a pillow in the crevice between the two double beds of an Anaheim Ramada Inn room. Though I couldn't see them, I knew my sister and Danny were on one of the two beds above us. From my vantage point, I could see a pyramid of Coors cans that had been constructed on the dresser. I reflexively searched for hangover symptoms before remembering that I hadn't been drinking. Allison and I had lingered down by the pool talking while Sarah and her friends partied in the room. We talked about career goals, hers mostly. I don't exactly know what mine are. She wants to be some kind of an engineer, either electrical or chemical, that choice being one of the few decisions she's yet to make. She said that growing up she'd planned to be a lawyer, but that now she wanted to start making money—lots of money—right out of college, not after three additional years of law school. We kissed last night by the pool when we ran out of things to say.

I raised myself up on my elbow and brushed Allison's hair from her face. I kissed her lips. She woke up and kissed me back.

Houston, Sophomore Year

Dub's sister, Sylvia, was a freshman at Rice, but she was often home. Sylvia had a dorm room—Rice requires its freshmen to live on campus—but her potluck roommate, flush with the freedom of college life and only recently paroled from a fundamentalist upbringing, liked towing home the occasional stray man. When she did, Sylvia returned to Clear Lake to sleep. She returned this evening to find Dub and me in some sort of late-round Twister lock, smooching in front of MTV.

"Great," Sylvia said, startling us by plunking her purse down on the coffee table. "I leave my roommate and Mr. Goodbar only to find my sister auditioning for work as a contortionist."

Dub French-kissed me once more to make what I was sure was an immature point, then spoke to her sister. "We were just talking—"

"I see," said Sylvia, channel-surfing without our permission.

"—about who would make a good sponsor for GOD. Stokes dissolved us until we find one. We got in some trouble today."

Sylvia flipped to *Saturday Night Live*.

"You oughta ask Sky—Mr. Waters," answered Sylvia,

uninterested in what kind of trouble we might have gotten into. "He's the best teacher at Grace. That's not saying much, really, but Sky's great. He treats you like there may be more going on inside you than, say, deciding what to wear to a deb ball. I don't know if he would do it, though. I don't think he's big into the Grace clubs and organizations scene. You should have Missy ask him though. He's particularly fond of girls."

"His name's really Sky?" I asked.

"I think they started calling him that when he first started teaching. His students in the eighties called him Skywaters, after Luke Skywalker. They said that he used the Force to determine grades. They couldn't figure out how else he did it. He never graded their assignments."

Sylvia plopped down on the couch with the finality of one who would move no more to escape the passion of others. I told Dub I ought to take off.

"Don't leave because of me, Steve," Sylvia said unconvincingly.

I stood to go. Dub got up as well. She stuffed her hands in my back pockets and pressed her ear against my back.

"Slut," Sylvia said.

"Jealous," Dub shot back.

I put on my heavy trench coat. This would be my last day in the near-freezing Houston December. I was flying out to San Diego for two weeks with my mother. For the first time since my parents' split, I wasn't anxious to see her, unsure as I was about my ability to function without Dub. Dub wore only a T-shirt and sweatpants, but she burrowed into the expanse of my coat and walked barefoot out to my car with me. She pressed me into the door of the El C, stood on her tiptoes, and kissed me—the perfect image of a World War

II—era taxi dancer smooching a lonely sailor down at the USO. There was something I had been wanting to tell her.

"I love you," I said.

"You love this car."

"That's different."

"We'll see."

San Diego, Senior Year

Toby the Party and I were in the same economics class together. This meant little, as T. P. rarely bothered to show, though he was here today in body if not spirit. We were supposed to be working on a graph showing the difference between the debt and the deficit, but I saw Toby's toe tapping and then noticed the wire leading from his book bag on the floor to small earplug headphones. He was listening to his Walkman.

I finished my graph early and decided to help out Toby with my free time. When I looked across the aisle, though, Toby was shuddering. I knew this epileptic kid in junior high who shook like this right before he went into a fit. I grabbed Toby's shoulder.

"Toby! What's up, man? You're freaking."

"He's dead. They're saying it on the radio. He's dead."

"Who's dead?"

Toby turned to face me. His eyes had watered up. "Kurt Cobain is dead. He blew his own head off."

By lunch the whole school knew. In the parking lot everyone rolled down their windows and blasted the station that was playing nothing but Nirvana. I sat in the El C by myself. Toby was staggering from car to car. Eventually he approached mine.

"We're having a wake on the beach tonight. You'll see the fire."

●●●

That night I could see the fire from my bedroom window. I slipped my *In Utero* CD in my Discman and made my way toward the light. There were nearly fifty of us by the time I got there. As I made my way into the circle I heard someone saying that she thought Kurt Cobain was a prophet and that he had died for our sins. Then this white guy with really skanky dreadlocks said that he thought it was set up to look like a suicide, but that the government wanted him dead because he had too much power. I turned my Discman all the way up and stared away from the fire out into the ocean. I felt a hand on my shoulder. It was Toby. He looked ghoulish. His pupils were black nickels, and I couldn't tell if he recognized me. He handed me the joint that was in his hand. I pushed my earphones forward so I could hear him speak.

"You know what he said in his note?" I shook my head no. "He quoted that song, 'It's better to burn out than to fade away.' That's so true, man. So true."

I pushed the earphones back. In my ears I heard the words, "I'm not like them, but I can pretend." I handed the joint back to Toby. He didn't notice I hadn't taken a hit.

On the way back to my house I threw the CD as far out into the Pacific as I could.

Houston, Sophomore Year

A good portion of my next paycheck from the Cineplex went toward paying off the long distance charges Dub and I racked up over the Christmas holidays. She picked me up at the airport when I returned from San Diego and drove me straight home. The astronaut, thankfully, was at work. I would try to avoid an introduction scene for as long as I could. I carried my bags up to my bedroom and Dub followed. She surveyed the monastic austerity of my bedroom's decor.

"I really like what you've done in here, Sport. It's just as I would have—"

I didn't let her finish. For three hours on the plane I'd anticipated this moment. Wrapping one arm around her waist and one hand around her neck, I think I actually— though without forethought—growled when I first kissed her. I backed her up to the bed, and when her feet could retreat no farther, she fell back with me on top of her.

"Miss me much?" she asked.

I reached down and began untucking her shirt.

"Hey, buddy," Dub began. Her lips were touching mine as she spoke. "We're heading into new territory here."

"I know." It was *completely* new for me. Dub and I had only kissed. Sure we had ground our hips together until I feared the friction would ignite our blue jeans, or worse, cause elephantiasis, but I had never ventured inside girls' clothing before. I wasn't quite sure how it operated. I felt like a slave, though, to the ghosts of all men who had gone forth before me and multiplied. This was chemistry, conditioning, history, instinct. I had no idea where I was going, but I was in a big hurry to get there. Left with no choice but to follow the compass needle in my boxers, I slid a hand over my girlfriend's stomach until I cupped the satiny fabric covering her right breast. I heard her inhale through wet teeth. Taking this as a positive sign, I squeezed. I began moving my thumb back and forth across her nipple like a windshield wiper. It firmed with each swipe. Dub gripped my blue jean pockets, and I sent my tongue on a journey to her ear and then down her neck.

Laundry room . . . predivorce . . . talking to Mom . . . watching her fold clothes . . . there had been a bra. Think, Steve, think. Ah yes. I remember now. A clasp, maybe two, in the back.

I slid my hand under Dub and began tracing the fabric of her bra. When I got to her spine, I intensified my search for any bump or node that would identify the hook mechanism. I tried to disguise my fumbling as some sort of exotic foreplay involving the lower shoulder blade erogenous zone.

"Want some help?"

"Please," I answered pitifully.

She brought her hands up to the front of her bra, to a spot between her breasts, and with a swift twist (I should have asked her to demonstrate this slowly), she unhooked herself. Quickly we were out of our shirts, naked from the waist up, and pressed against each other. Dub rolled me over on my back and straddled me. She kissed my forehead first, then my lips, then my neck. In the process her nipples skimmed along the surface of my chest, and I luxuriated in the unearthly smoothness of female breasts against my skin. I felt a dangerous tingle, but the sound of the automatic garage door opening interrupted any worries I had of embarrassing myself.

"Shit, shit, shit, shit, shit," I said, as I rolled out from under Dub and onto the floor.

Dub calmly began putting her clothes back on. My first attempt to do the same resulted in the label of my T-shirt serving as a bib for my Adam's apple.

"Try that again," Dub said, running her fingers through her tangled hair.

I turned my T-shirt right side out and remembered to keep the label in back as I refrocked. I could hear the astronaut coming up the stairs. I wanted to throw up. Dub sat down at my desk just as the astronaut entered the room.

"We just got here. We just got back from the airport," I said without being asked.

"Hello, Wanda," he said. "How have you been?"

"Good."

"Steve, I need to see you after Wanda leaves. I'll be in my office." Then he left.

Dub mouthed "uh-oh" from across the room. "I probably ought to get out of here," she said as she came toward me. "It didn't sound like he was willing to wait too long for that little chat."

"I keep forgetting that you were friends with Sarah."

"Still am."

"So you've been over before?"

"Plenty of times. We never really hung out here, though. It's not exactly fun central, you know? You suppose he wants to talk to you about that?" She pointed to my bed. Waves of comforter leapt out from a human-sized indention in the middle. I shrugged. Dub kissed me quickly on the cheek. "Hang tough. It was worth it for me." She showed herself the way out. I collected myself before entering the astronaut's sanctum.

"You wanted to see me?"

The astronaut sat at his desk, facing away from me. He wore his reading glasses. Stacks of documents bound in red and green pressboard were spread out in front of him. I knew, without looking, they were classified reports. Before he went to bed, the astronaut would lock them in the poorly disguised end table/safe. He closed the report in his hands, but he didn't turn around.

"I don't want you upstairs with Wanda—or any girl for that matter—when I'm not home."

"We weren't doing anything."

"That's not the issue. There's no reason for her to be upstairs with you. It's not appropriate. That's my final decision."

And that, I believe, was our longest conversation in a year.

San Diego, Senior Year

Allison and I have seen each other every day this week. I haven't invited her to join me at Cap's yet. I don't know that I will. I need these three hours a day—to write, to screw my head on straight, to drink coffee and pretend I'm in college.

I think DeMouy is on to us. This, despite our scant acknowledgment of each other's existence at school. Allison says he asks how I'm doing when he talks to her. He never asks me how she's doing, but I can't say this offends me.

I understand now why Allison is so preoccupied with making money. After a romantic night on the beach cuddling by a driftwood fire, she explained her current living situation. (I took great pains, incidentally, to make the fire appear unplanned, though I had, earlier in the day, gathered the wood, soaked it in lighter fluid, and surrounded it with skull-sized boulders.)

Allison was eleven and living in a house not far down the beach from where we sat. She was waiting impatiently for her brother and mother to return from grocery shopping. She had won the fifty-meter backstroke in a swim meet that morning, and she couldn't wait to show off her ribbon. (She leaned away from me at this point and stared out into the ocean.) She said the phone rang, and she answered it. Her uncle asked to speak to her father. Her father got on the phone, and Allison watched as his knees buckled and he collapsed against the refrigerator. He dropped the phone, and, unsure of what she could do, eleven-year-old Allison ran to help. Her father wrapped her in his arms and rocked her for half an hour before telling her that her mother and brother had been killed by a drunk driver on the drive home from the store.

When we go to my house, Allison makes me detour around the crash site. She says she still has nightmares, but other than that, she's a mentally healthy, if not constantly happy, girl. Her father, on the other hand, has never fully recovered. He tried going back to work for his defense contractor employer, but after months of missing deadlines, disappearing from the office, and, finally, intentionally sabotaging his company's latest mass death weapon, he was fired. The two of them lived for a couple years on insurance money and savings, but after that income had been depleted, they had to sell the house. Allison says she hopes she's making enough money to support her father by the time that money runs out. In the meantime, she's been the housekeeper, gardener, cook, and sole companion to him.

"I've nearly convinced him to join a therapy group for people who have lost their spouses," she tells me before laying her head across my lap and staring into the radiant embers of the fire. Sitting there, I remembered a conversation I'd had with Dub. She had tried to convince me that, when you're young, you're more compatible with people different from you. For the first time, I thought she might be right about that.

Allison thinks her father would consider any boy she brought home a threat, and I don't care to push it. I'm happy with the way things are. I told Allison the story of my messy life. After hearing about hers, mine didn't seem worthy of secrecy.

Houston, Sophomore Year

Months passed without a member of GOD mentioning the need for a new sponsor. The fact that the school didn't recognize our existence had only heightened our smugness.

"We're mainland China, man," Doug insisted to no one in particular and everyone in general, "the baddest boys on the block, recognized or not."

"Everyone—except Taiwan maybe—has recognized the Peoples' Republic of China by now," Matt mentioned.

"Spare me the details, Ivy!" Doug said scornfully.

That was before the yearbook staff announced group photos for the yearbook would be taken the week before spring break. Suddenly Doug was anxious for the sanctions to end. Five hundred dollars, after all, rode on our inclusion. All GODists had taken to eating under the only tree on the school grounds that wasn't a staked sapling—a sycamore in the courtyard between the English and art wings. We were on a split lunch schedule, so I saw only half the membership.

"What are we going to do about a sponsor?" Doug asked sullenly.

"I say screw 'em. We're mainland China," Dub answered, not being much help.

"What about Mr. Waters? I think he's an English teacher," I said, remembering Sylvia's suggestion.

"Man, I don't know," said Ivy. "I've heard he's a freak."

That settled it for Doug. If Ivy said he was a freak, the man was in. "He must be perfect."

Veg got up from the grass and patted pita crumbs off of his turquoise wool Mexican Baja. "I'll go try to find out where his classroom is." And Doug's latest yes-man was on his way.

It turned out that Mr. Waters' classroom was segregated from the rest of the English department. Room B16 used the space between an industrial trades (shop) class and a family solutions (unwed mothers) class. Because his classroom was smaller than the breakfast nooks of most Clear Lake homes, Waters had given the space a modicum of openness by removing all desks other than his own, which he tucked in a corner. A score of navy blue plastic chairs were arranged roughly in a circle in the middle of the room. Behind his desk, a poster of the cover of Bruce Springsteen's *Born to Run* stretched from the ceiling to the floor. The rest of the wall was covered with a comparably sized flag of Scotland. On the chalkboard, he had written, "A writer is somebody for whom writing is more difficult than it is for other people." —Thomas Mann.

Waters was sticking chunks of banana in his mouth as our half dozen entered his room. He also had a thermos cup full of stew and a Koala kiwi-lime-grapefruit soda resting on an unfolded cloth napkin. He appraised us as we encircled his desk.

"Mr. Waters, do you have a minute? We're the Grace Order of Dadaists." It must have sounded ludicrous, like we were witnessing door to door, hoping for converts.

"Ah, yes, the infamous—" (That made us feel good.) He wiped his mouth. "And outlawed, from what I hear."

"That's what we're here to see you about," our leader said. "We need a sponsor to get rerecognized."

"Why would a group of such obviously secure trend-buckers like yourselves need official status, anyway? Doesn't your banning only serve your image as young iconoclasts?"

"I'm not sure," Doug said. "What's an iconoclast?"

"You need to take my class; you'd know these things," Waters said. "An iconoclast is someone who debunks the platitudes mainstream society espouses: 'Elvis is king,' 'Love is forever,' 'My country, right or wrong.' "

"So what you're saying," Dub said, "is that an iconoclast probably wouldn't show up panting for a yearbook picture party."

"Goes without saying," Waters said.

But he accepted our offer. He had been out of the good graces of the school's administration for so long—hence the trial-size classroom—that he figured sponsoring us could do no further damage. When he actually got out of his chair at one point to see us out, it seemed as though never-ending limbs just kept issuing from below the desk. He must have been six-foot-six, but he was, as well, the only human at Grace who could make me seem husky. He looked spidery and breakable, his bony features accentuated by a pointy goatee and piked nose. His mustache was of the wispy sort favored by cast members of *Godspell*. Though his coarse, dark hair was graying slightly, his wrinkle-free face led me to believe he'd yet to see thirty-five.

I didn't show up for yearbook photos, but Dub had a friend on the yearbook staff who smuggled us out an extra print. Each member of the group packed a clawed red hammer. They had crossed their arms across their chests, their hammers in their right hand. No one smiled, except Lynnette. I realized after gazing at the picture for a couple minutes that they were all doing something peculiar with their free hands. I asked Dub what it was.

"Sign language," she said. Sure enough, when I gazed even closer I could tell each of their hands formed a letter.

"So what does it spell?"

"Depends on how you read it. Forwards it says 'Dog was star.' "

"So backwards it spells . . ."

" 'Rats saw God.' "

Waters, in his first official duty since signing our charter as club sponsor, supplied the G.

San Diego, Senior Year

This had to be a joke. Sarah wouldn't really do this to me, would she?

But here I was, lying on the couch, Allison spooned against my stomach, watching *The Right Stuff*—my sister's video rental choice—three hours on the heroics of our first space explorers. Danny and Sarah shared the BarcaLounger. A mixing bowl of microwaved Redenbacher's rested on the coffee table between us. Despite Sarah's original vow that our first double date would be our last, the four of us had ended up in similar positions on more than a few occasions. Neither Allison nor I were much for going out, plus, the more I got to know Danny, the better I liked him. He could make Sarah shut up. She was positively gaga for him. From what Mom said, Danny was the first boy for whom Sarah wasn't the puppet master. Mom, though she would never admit it, had grown fond of Danny. He almost charmed her into making an appearance at a "Skinheads Against Racism" rally he helped organize.

Good group chemistry alone, however, was not going to convince me to watch this movie.

"Is this the only thing you rented?" I asked rather pointedly when I saw the title come up on the screen.

"Yeah," she said defensively. "You got a problem with that?"

"Didn't you get enough of this bullshit growing up?"

"Bitch, bitch, bitch, bitch, bitch . . ."

Now I was pissed. "You could have watched this on your own any day since you were first able to put a tape in the machine by yourself. God knows it was made available to us. Didn't the astronaut put a copy of it in your Christmas stocking one year?"

"He put it in yours."

Oh yeah. "The point is, why do we have to watch it now? We've heard all these stories before. I'll bet you firemen's families don't go out renting *Backdraft* for kicks."

Sarah used the television remote control to turn up the volume. The VCR control, however, was within my reach. I paused the opening credits of the movie.

"You are a son of a bitch," Sarah said, now pissed. "Look, you've hardly talked to Dad in a year, and you won't have to see him until the wedding, which is still months away. Can't you just shut up and watch the movie?"

"I don't have to see him then, either. Who said I was going to the wedding?"

"He's asked you to be the best man," she said incredulously.

"And I didn't say yes." I sat up. I thought it important to look stern when I explained this to Sarah. "You were so young when they split up, and you see so little of the astronaut, you don't understand the man. He just wants me there to put on a show. It would look good. I don't know, maybe cute, or something, to have me standing there beside him. I'm not going to do it."

Sarah lost it. She hopped out of her chair and began screaming at me and wagging her finger in my face. "You're the one who doesn't understand anything. You're the one who can't remember, or is too dumb to figure out, why they broke up. You just see what you want to see."

I had no idea what she was talking about, but Allison and Danny were obviously uncomfortable. Danny was looking out the window; Allison inspected her palms. I had no desire to continue this in front of them.

"Fine, fine, whatever you say. Let's not get into this here."

Then she reached across the coffee table and slapped me. When she spoke again, she was difficult to understand because she was sobbing.

"You are so stupid. You don't even see it, do you? You are just like him. You won't put up a fight because you're so afraid of being embarrassed, just like him. You are just as meticulous as he is. You expect everyone else around you to be perfect. You don't forgive anyone. You open envelopes like they're priceless. You make your bed like you're sealing food. You've probably even convinced yourself that you're not looking more and more like him each day. It's a good thing you wear those earrings so we can tell the two of you apart. Neither of you trust anyone but yourselves. No, that's not true. You trust Mom. Dad did, too, at one point, and look what it got him."

I wanted to disappear, but what the hell did she mean about Mom? "What are you saying?"

"Haven't you ever wondered how Mom managed to meet someone so fast? Did you know she got married on the first day she legally could after the divorce was final? Did you know Chuck is from Cocoa Beach? You weren't the only one who listened at vents in that house."

"Watch what you're saying, Sarah. You can't mean what . . ."

"Look, believe what you want, but just remember, you sat there grinning like an idiot at Mom and Chuck's wedding. You were so pleased, like somehow Mom was getting back at Dad for putting her through so many years of hardship."

The VCR took itself off Pause after the long delay. The volume had been left at its previous deafening level. The sound of jet engines filled the family room. F-14s left white streaks across our big screen TV as they disappeared into the horizon. Sarah wiped her eyes. Visual display bars blinked off one by one as she brought the volume of the movie down to a decent level.

"You don't even call him your father. I am so sick of that."

She sat back down with Danny. I just kept my eyes fixed on the screen. Allison grabbed my hand and pulled me back to my previous position on the couch. She pulled my arm around her and squeezed it hard against her body. For the next three hours I had to remind myself to breathe.

Houston, Sophomore Year

My entire second semester at Grace fell into a precise weekly schedule that varied only on the odd weekend that Dub would visit relatives in Shreveport or spend the night with Sylvia at the Rice dorms. Normally, I would pick Dub up for school. Walk her to her classes. Drive through Taco Bell or Burger King for lunch under the sycamore (lately called the Joshua Tree by GOD). Hang out at Dub's until it was time to go to work. On nights I had off, we rented movies or went swimming in the Pleasant Woods Estates pool after it closed. We would hop the waist-high fence and make out in the dark water. Every time she went partying with her sister, ultimately crashing at her place, I would pace the projection room at work and envision poetry-citing, acne-free college men offering my girlfriend mixed drinks and asking her what her major was.

"You should hook up with Doug after you get off. You're usually out by eleven. Do something with your friends," Dub would say.

"I don't want to. I want to be with you."

"You're too cute," she would say.

Besides, Doug was always in the same place—his garage, practicing with Veg and Bill. The Grippe was readying for stardom. The Chappell garage had become the center of the GOD universe; Missy and Rhonda, Samantha and Holly, Zipper and Virginia—they'd all drop in, report on parties, and fawn over the boys in the band. I didn't feel much a part of it.

The only topic of conversation around the Joshua Tree for two weeks prior to spring break was the Galveston condominium owned by Holly's family. Her parents told her that she and a few of her friends could use the condo over the break. Naturally, her parents assumed these friends would be female, but they had never specifically made that distinction. So when Holly invited all of GOD to spend spring break with Samantha and her, it set off a string of lies on my part: lies at work, lies to the astronaut. I managed to get three consecutive days off at the Cineplex for my "chemotherapy." The astronaut believed I would be staying at the Whitesides' and that the parents would be with us. I couldn't, however, trade shifts on the first Friday and Saturday of the break. Dub headed to Galveston with Rhonda and Missy and without me.

I drove down early Sunday morning. Ivy answered my 10 A.M. knock on the condo door. Beer bottles, sticky blenders, empty bags of chips, and comatose male bodies were strewn across the floor of the living room that faced the beach. Ivy was the only one awake. He had already scrambled eggs, which he offered to share, and was eating in front of a muted TV. Cooler teenagers than us were frolicking in Daytona on MTV's exclusive coverage of spring break tan line contests. I asked him where Dub was sleeping, and he pointed to the appropriate door. All three musketeers—Dub, Missy, Rhonda—were sleeping on the king-sized bed that filled the room. Fortunately, Dub was closest to the door. Had she anticipated my Prince Charming intentions? I kneeled down beside the bed and kissed her on the lips. I tasted the stale, fermented tang of beer mouth. No, she had slept where she had fallen.

I slipped my hand underneath the sheets and ran it down the warm cotton T-shirt that ended where her panties began. I rode my hand over her butt and down along her thigh. She murmured. I brought my ear closer to her, so I could hear. This time it was clear.

"Sergio," she cooed.

Then she grabbed me and bit my ear.

"That's what you get for being a perv."

● ● ●

Later that day, I played my first game of football since I was eight and first grasped the import of the activity to the astronaut. He had told me to pull my head out after I dropped a pass in some meaningless two-on-two matchup with neighborhood kids. I didn't catch a pass the rest of the day, but I'll say this for the man, he kept throwing them.

Here, on vacation with friends, things would be different. The Whiteside brothers and I matched up against Doug, Veg, and Missy for a game of beach two below. I wasn't sure whether Doug took Missy as a concession for our team having me or Ivy, but I resolved not to take it personally. Our foes jumped out to a quick touchdown lead. On the opening kickoff Missy ran in—and I'll use this term literally—*unmolested* for the score. I had her dead to rights, but I couldn't figure out where to touch her.

"On her ass, you wuss," Dub shouted from the sidelines.

We got killed due largely to the fact that Doug took the game eighteen times more seriously than the rest of us, at one point stiff-arming Ivy into a sand dune and then Electric-Sliding across the back of the end zone. I caught a few more passes that bounced off my chest, so I was happy. When Bill decided he wanted to run some routes, I discovered I had a congenital talent for throwing a tight spiral. I hit Bill on a couple of sideline streaks that dropped in over his outside shoulder just beyond Doug's flailing arms. The late TDs made the score a bit more respectable.

For one glorious day I answered to the nickname "Moon," who I was told quarterbacked for the Oilers.

"He's just the only one out here not hungover," Doug said.

"Okay, when you're feeling better, you can show us your arm," Bill said sarcastically.

That night we built a huge bonfire on the beach. We sang "Kum Ba Yah" just to be smartasses. Hundreds of high school and college students along the beach joined us in our rendition. By the time we got to "Someone's shouting, Lord," we could have been led on a crusade. Samantha, sitting directly across the fire from me, had put on a sweatshirt when the night turned chilly, but she was still in her bikini bottom. The more I drank the less capable of averting my gaze I became. I don't think anyone noticed, but it got me thinking about those medieval monks who would whip themselves for impure thoughts about stable boys and the round earth theory. If I had a cat-o'-nine-tails, I would have had at me right then. I was in love with the girl under the blanket with me.

I don't know how many backroom deals Dub had to

make with Missy and Rhonda to convince them to sleep on the floor somewhere else in the house that night, but we ended up getting the extra bedroom to ourselves.

"Have you thought at all about birth control?" Dub asked when we were down to our underwear. We hadn't progressed beyond this point, and the truth was no, I hadn't. Dub asked the question so frankly, though, I felt stupid for not having considered it.

"A bit," I lied.

"Think about it some more."

That night we wrapped ourselves together, safe in our underwear, a little drunk, and I forgot all about the astronaut . . . Doug . . . Samantha . . . condoms and spermicides . . . French words for common American expressions . . . the numerical value of pi.

Houston, Summer Before Junior Year

More than any holiday, the last day of school usually served to bump up my enthusiasm thermostat from detachment to a point just shy of zeal. The last day of my sophomore year, however, failed to measure up to its predecessors. Three months in San Diego without Dub? Get real. I was, by nature, mopey. Forlorn and mopey was going to be an ugly combination.

As soon as my Friday night shift ended at the 'Plex, I headed to Doug's. Graduation was the next evening, but I would be on a plane for the West Coast by then. That night I said my final good-byes to Trey, Bill, Holly, and Samantha. When I arrived, The Grippe was rehearsing and was well into a raucous rendition of Alice Cooper's "School's Out." Veg's vocals somehow managed to incorporate both the nasal, emotionally desolated yowl of Bob Mould and the requisite "we mean it, maaaaan!" snarl of late seventies punk. I noticed that, though the band still unleashed vision-blurring torrents of sound, they were no longer merely loud. They stomped through the song with none of the volume-over-ability bluster that was their early tendency. They had gigs booked at Zelda's and the Vatican that I would miss. Even this made me sad despite my worsening relationship with Doug. It's like he took it as a blow to his ego that I wanted to spend as much time as possible with Dub. After I said I didn't want to be in the band, he quit asking me if I wanted to do anything. He even referred to Dub as "your wife." The more shit he dished out, the less I saw of him.

Later I sat next to Bill and Holly, dangling my pallid legs in the pool. Holly was heading for Northwestern in a matter of days; she had enrolled in the first summer session. Bill had been accepted by MIT. The two had been a couple since their sophomore year.

"I know it's none of my business," I said when Dub went into the house to use the bathroom, "but how are you going to do it, stay together, when you're so far apart?"

Holly looked at Bill and something passed between them I couldn't interpret. Holly answered. "We're going to see other people in college. We're breaking up without the big fight, or the prefight, or the thirty-day make-each-other-miserable period. I'm not saying I won't want to call him every day, and he'll probably die without me, but why ruin something so perfect by trying to stay together?"

It was logic I simply didn't understand, but I kept my mouth shut.

San Diego, Senior Year

I carried the stack of letters waiting for me on the kitchen bar up to my room. Since my fight with Sarah, I had been ducking the rest of my family. What she said, it just couldn't be true. Still, I didn't look my mom in the eye and I had to fight the urge to take one of Chuck's dumbbells to the side of his head. Sarah, she would want to talk about it, or worse, apologize. Give me some time. I'll deal.

My mail came exclusively from colleges: Pepperdine, accepted; Loyola Marymount, accepted; UCLA, accepted. The fourth letter bore the embossed crimson insignia of Harvard. Why did the verdict contained in this envelope loom so large? Because the astronaut never did this. He never got accepted to an Ivy League school, to conceivably the preeminent school in the country. Remembering Sarah's derisive comments about my letter-opening mastery, I examined the envelopes I had already opened. All of them survived undamaged. I could send them back to the schools for a deposit. I held the Harvard envelope up to the light. No help. I ripped it open. The envelope tore surgically down the bottom crease. Sighing, I reduced it to confetti. Then I unfolded the letter: Harvard, accepted.

Spreading my arms and extending my fingers, I nodded my head and used my hands to settle the thundering audience. I mouthed thank yous into an invisible microphone.

I didn't even have to pull a drowning woman out of a river.

If this was good news for me, it was better for Allison. She scored twenty points higher on her SAT; she participated in more activities; she made significantly better grades. She was a shoo-in. It didn't matter in any real sense. She needed to go somewhere on a full ride, but she had cared enough about the results to spend fifty dollars on the application fee. She probably got her acceptance today, too. I called her at home.

"Kimble residence," she said. What a square.

"It's me. Heard from Harvard yet?"

"Last week," she said.

"And?"

" 'We sincerely regret to inform you, yadda, yadda, yadda.' " She paused. "Why? Did you get your letter yet?"

"Yeah. My letter just had two words on it—Charlie Vato."

"Yeah, well, Harvard sucks," she said.

"Harvard *does* suck," I agreed.

We talked for a few more minutes before hanging up. I considered Harvard and why they had green-lighted me. I had been wrong about the astronaut never getting accepted there. He just was.

San Diego/Houston,
Summer Before Junior Year

I flew back to Texas once that summer. It was during this visit that Dub and I lost our virginity. After the mental anguish I suffered buying condoms, I would have felt pretty stupid had we not done the deed. Sex, in the clinical rather than the rhapsodic sense, had been the prime topic of most of our daily phone calls. Would we? Should we? Dub was a regular medical expert by the time all was said and done. I had to change my flight arrangements once, because I would have arrived at her most fertile time of the month. We briefly discussed the pill.

"Let's see," she said. "I'll experience radical mood swings. I'll get nauseous—probably gain weight." There was a pause on the phone. "It'll make my boobs bigger."

"I say go for it."

But she hadn't. She offered to purchase the condoms

herself, but that made no sense. People knew her in Clear Lake. I was satisfactorily unheard-of in San Diego. Besides, this was a man's job. The deal went down at a Piggly Wiggly on my fifty-minute lunch hour. Dub made me promise not to buy them from a gas station bathroom vending machine.

"No fancy colors, no feathers, no glow-in-the-dark feature, nothing that says, 'for her pleasure.' " Dub instructed. "Something with a spermicide . . . and Sylvia says the lubricated kind are better."

"You asked your sister what kind of rubber we should use?"

"Big sisters have to tell you these things; it's in their contract."

I made up my mind that I would make this purchase without any of the stock comic antics of others in my position. I wouldn't pay for the condoms along with a plethora of nonessential, unsexy food—frozen Tater Tots, nondairy creamer, allspice—as if the variety would prevent a checker from noticing the virginal boy at the counter aiming to have sex. Nope. I planned on swaggering up to the express line, standing feet shoulder-width, gripping my fist with the opposite hand behind my back, daring the checker to notice my crotch.

Initially thrown by the selection offered by the contraceptive industry, I became conscious of the eternity I'd been gazing at the condom rack. I wondered briefly if I would eventually develop some form of brand loyalty. I finally selected a box of twelve—any less would have seemed superficial and cheap; any more would have come off narcissistic. There was no line at the express counter. The cashier was roughly my mom's age. She scanned the box, demanded the money, gave me change—all without so much as reviewing the instructions for use or questioning my moral rectitude.

I flew back to Texas on my seventeenth birthday. The midsummer trip was requiring a significant chunk out of my savings, but I didn't care. As I hustled off the plane and up the tunnel, I was blindsided by my eager girlfriend who bear-hugged me, knocked me into the tunnel wall, and effectively halted the deplaning process. The money was already worth it.

"Happy birthday, baby," she gushed, trying out a fresh pet name.

Despite making out at every red light and stopping at the astronaut's to drop off my luggage, we eventually arrived at Dub's place. The sun was just beginning to set when we got there, but the temperature would probably not dip below the century mark for another couple months. I was surprised to find us alone in the air-conditioned sanctuary of the house.

"They'll be gone for hours. I've sent them to the movies."

I tried to imagine the astronaut's reaction had I attempted shooing him off so I could have the house to myself and my girlfriend. Dub took my hand and led me, not to the bedroom as expected, but to the dining room table already set for two. The cloth-lined basket of French bread, lead crystal decanter of petite sirah, white tapers in a silver candelabra, and expensive-looking China clued me in: Dub had cooked. She lit the candles with a long wooden match which she withdrew from a decanter. Her hand trembled nervously as she did so. She dimmed the lights and instructed me to pour the wine. She disappeared for a moment before I heard Nat King Cole's voice come purring in through the room's speakers.

I filled both glasses like a regular Don Juan, took my first sip, and remembered that I didn't like wine. It always tasted bitter and made all the moisture on my tongue evaporate. I could hear oven and refrigerator doors rasping open and slamming shut as well as the scraping of utensils against dishes. She returned carrying a bowl of fettuccine Alfredo and a platter with two breasts of chicken Parmesan. She set them down, took a sip of her own wine, circled the table, hugged me from behind, and returned to her seat.

"Happy birthday," she announced proudly. "Now eat."

And I tried. I really tried, but . . .

It's difficult, really, deciding where to start on this: the Alfredo sauce had congealed on top of the soggy noodles to forge a chocolate dipped conelike shell; the insides of the chicken breasts were still registering a pulse while the breaded shell had achieved a driveway oil stain tint; the water-thin marinara sauce fled the breast and formed a pink sea surrounding Poultry Island in the middle of my plate. I kept my head bowed. I chewed and chewed, then chiseled off another bite, and continued to chew. I hadn't made much headway when I sensed that Dub had stopped eating and was watching me. I didn't look up though. I was afraid she would ask me how everything was.

"Please stop trying to eat this. I'll be even sadder if I have to rush you to the hospital," she said. I took in her face. A tear fell down to her monumental mouth. I thought she looked beautiful. "I suck. I wanted this to be perfect."

"It is. It's a perfect night."

"I love you," she said.

In saying so, she lessened my "I love you" lead to 946 to 1. She wiped her eyes and started laughing. "You don't even want to see the birthday cake." Covering her meal with her napkin, Dub stood. "Follow me," she said.

The double French doors of Dub's room were

uncurtained. They opened out to the patio that stretched across the back of the house and overlooked the back-yard. The lights were off in the bedroom, but the outside lights streamed through the door windows and allowed my eyes to adjust easily. Dub inserted a Lenny Kravitz cassette into her jambox.

"Come here," she directed from beside her bed. I stood before her, feeling suddenly young. Images of play-ing with Tonka dump trucks and running from cootied girls at recess played through my mind as Dub unbut-toned my shirt.

"Do you want to do this?" Dub asked.

"I think so."

We undressed each other as if the process would later be described in sonnets. Each garment removed, whether preciously draped over a chair or lustily cast to the floor, was a verse. Okay, the part involving shoe removal would have best been described in a limerick. I ended up standing naked from my ankles up, hopping on one foot, then the other, as Dub untied my Chuck Taylors and pulled each Levi leg over my foot. I wanted for all the world to have this act be the melding of two kindred souls, the uniting of two perfectly matched bodies, but I would have lost my balance. When Dub finally relieved me of my last shred of clothing, I resisted the urge to cover the titanium love barometer between my legs. Was it the right size? The right shape? The right color? Would Dub know whether it was? It was the first time she had seen it. She had rubbed it through my blue jeans, and we had goomed up my shorts dry humping until I thought I would die, but this was the first time Junior had the plea-sure of meeting a woman in the flesh. Dub gripped the shaft and gave it a couple preliminary tugs. I lost my breath.

"How does that feel?" she asked, genuinely curious.

In a moment of epiphany I realized that every sensual pleasure in my lifetime would be compared to this. How could I describe how sex felt when nothing so far— roller coasters, shower massages, coin-operated beds— approached this sensation. As a graying middle-ager I might describe landing a marlin as feeling like great sex, but right now, I sure couldn't tell Dub that what she was doing to me felt like catching a fish.

"Nice," I answered.

Mom fell in love with Warren Beatty in the movie *Splendor in the Grass.* After that, she never missed one of his flicks. We owned them all on videotape. Earlier during the summer, with little else to do, I watched most of the collection. In *Splendor,* Beatty plays an in-heat teenage boy (Is there any other kind?) cursed with a girlfriend, Natalie Wood, who won't round second base. She goes crazy; he marries a beautiful Spanish woman. That made sense. What terrified me was one of the mid-period Beatty offerings, *Shampoo.* In a final scene, we find Beatty putting it to Julie Christie on a guest house floor, his naked butt ramming away pistonlike. Strings don't swell. The director doesn't cut away to hands entwining. Unless you count "oh yes," no tender words were spoken. Watching it unfold, I had a flash. Maybe sex isn't indulging in each heartfelt caress. Maybe sex is friction, pure and simple.

These thoughts cluttered my mind as I loomed in push-up position over Dub's naked body. My triceps were going rubbery. I didn't quite understand the hold up here. Given the opportunity, I believe I could have used Junior to cut glass. I began doubting she had an orifice down there. Continuing to make what I hoped where sexy noises, I tried again. Brick wall. Dub sighed.

"Let's roll over," she said.

After trading positions, Dub began grinding into me.

As she did, the meeting point turned into this veritable tropical rain forest. She started breathing harder. I don't think I would have lasted through this had I not been sheathed in latex. Clumsily we charged toward lost innocence.

Dub raised her haunches and reached back between my legs. She positioned Junior in rocket ship perpendicularity and then lowered herself down onto me. I realized five or six seconds after the actual event that I was inside her, that I was no longer a virgin, that I would finally be allowed to hunt buffalo with the village elders. I could almost feel my complexion clearing up. For autobiographical accuracy, I noted the digital clock read 9:20. Now what? Dub started rocking back and forth. I attempted to thrust in a matching rhythm, but it seemed like every time she zigged, I zagged. Twice I fell out and had to be reinserted. That particular trick, at least, became easier to accomplish. After the second time, I convinced Dub that we should try this the old-fashioned way. Back on top, I became the master of my destiny. Initially I set a leisurely tempo, but as the pleasure index increased, so did my hip speed. Dub had both hands around my neck, and I gave up trying to gaze into her eyes during the act. I let my face sink into the pillow beside her shoulder. The condom I was wearing was numbing most sensation coming from the South Pole, but the peripheral stimulation was electric: the way our sweaty bodies were sliding across each other, Dub's fingernails digging into my neck, her irregular panting, the lemony scent of fabric softener on the pillowcases.

After years of self-service, I recognized the signs of impending orgasm—the tingle, the shortening of breath, my testicles' desire to join my lungs. I pushed myself up when I reached the point of no return. Dub's eyes were closed, and she was biting her lower lip. And then it was over. As I stopped my pushing and pulling, Dub's eyes opened.

"Did you?" she asked.

I nodded. She leaned up and kissed me tenderly. The clock read 9:26.

I put in two solid minutes of snuggling, but in the back of my mind I was reviewing the instructions that came with the box of condoms. There was more to proper use than I would have imagined. Take, for example, the sixth and final step. The manufacturer recommended that I grip the sides of the condom when I pulled out. The latex felt like such a second skin that I hardly believed we were in danger of it slipping off, but I did as instructed. I was surprised that the reservoir tip contained only a moderate amount of fluid. It felt like there should be a billiard ball–sized globe at the end. I walked naked and embarrassed to the bathroom adjoining Dub's room. There I removed the condom. Though it wasn't in the instructions, I tied off the end before flushing it down the commode. I didn't want some renegade sperm scaling the porcelain and slithering into bed with my partner.

I opened the door of the bathroom to find the lights had been turned on. Dub, dressed only in a T-shirt, sat across the room in a pink high-backed armless chair. She had wrapped her arms around her knees, drawing them up against her chest. Her eyes were the only part of her face I could see, and they weren't looking at me. My clothes, unfortunately, were on the opposite side of the bed closest to her.

"Do you know why the French call these armless chairs boudoir chairs?" Dub asked. I dove on the bed before answering in the negative. "It's because Louis *quatorze* liked boffing sitting down. He ordered armless chairs put in all the ladies' bedrooms at Versailles." I sat up at the edge of the bed, a corner of bedspread covering my privates, and fished for my boxers with my toes. Thankfully, Dub still wasn't looking at me in all my au naturel glory. Louis *quatorze*, I guessed, would have paraded to his underwear, commanded the satisfied noblewoman to salute his manhood, or quite possibly, simply exited naked. Suddenly Dub looked at me. I blushed. I felt I should say something.

"Funny. We didn't get that particular lesson in French."

"Do you feel any different?"

"No. What about you?"

"I feel sad. Like I've closed a door behind me and I'll never be able to go back. Like my dad doesn't have to love me anymore." She rocked herself back and forth in her chair. "And it really wasn't as big a deal as I thought it would be."

Then I was in a hurry to leave. Abandoning the safety of the bed, I collected my clothes and dressed quickly. I was gone before her parents came home. She didn't try to make me stay.

We saw each other the next day and tried to pretend it hadn't happened. We reenacted our Galveston road trip, but we didn't kiss with the same ferocity, and we didn't try quite as hard to impress each other. I flew back to California with eleven condoms to my name.

San Diego, Senior Year

Allison was in Palo Alto, visiting Stanford. Had I remembered Mom and Chuck were having a party that Friday, I would have endured the free verse and cloves of a late night at Cap's. The living room and deck bustled with pilots, stewardesses, and real estate agents. They seemed to get on famously. I tried slipping into the kitchen to snake some of

the Hawaiian meatballs Mom always makes when she enter-
tains. I was cut off by a sun-bleached blonde.

"Here he is! Here he is, Cindy! You're right. I hardly recognize him. Why he's such a young *man*." The
woman, a few fuzzy navels over her limit, motioned for
my mother, then she turned back around. "I'll bet you
don't even recognize me." She was right. Others crowded into the kitchen pivoted to regard me. I swear, the
empathy was palpable. "Maybe this will refresh your
memory."

Then the woman grabbed my shoulders, pulled me
down to her level (literally and figuratively), and kissed me.
If I was initially dismayed, think of how I felt when her
tongue came swishing past my teeth.

"Judy! Stop that! You are going to embarrass him to
death. He's too young for you, and besides, he has a girlfriend." The voice was my mom's and the tone was jovial but
unequivocal. "Son, are you okay? You must remember Judy.
She used to be our receptionist at the office."

A lightbulb. It was the ghost of office parties past. "I
remember you now." I didn't mean it humorously, but the
crowd chuckled anyway. Judy seemed unoffended. Mom
went around the circle introducing me to co-workers of hers
and Chuck's. I didn't remember a single name by the time
she finished.

"Steve's graduating next month," Mom announced.

"Where are you going to college? USC's looking for
some go-getters," said a pilot. He punched my shoulder
with the side of his fist. I mentally nixed any possible future
as a Trojan.

"Didn't I see a letter from Harvard the other day?"
Mom asked, either blindly optimistic or unintentionally

insensitive. "What did they have to say?"

"Don't call us. We'll call you," I said. The audience shifted uncomfortably and returned to their conversations after this bad news.

"Oh, honey, who needs Harvard, anyway? Plenty of schools still want you."

"I'll survive," I said. I tested, with meatballs, the sturdiness of a paper plate, then escaped to my room. Even a closed door couldn't protect me from the blasting of the *Sleepless in Seattle* soundtrack. I dragged the cord of my telephone into my closet and shut the door, affording myself some silence. I dialed the 713 area code, then with a little difficulty, the remaining seven digits. The astronaut answered groggily. I had forgotten the two-hour time difference and the old man's adherence to *Poor Richard's Almanac.*

"Sorry I'm calling so late."

"No problem. What's up?"

"I just wanted to let you know that I can make the wedding."

"Steve, that's super. Jacqueline's excited about seeing you again."

Why did he have to put it that way? "One other thing. I'm graduating June third. I get four tickets, and I've got one left." He didn't speak. "I'll leave it at the auditorium window . . . if you can make it. If you can't, that's fine."

"I'll see what I can do."

We said light-speed good-byes and hung up.

Houston, Summer Before Junior Year

I returned to Texas the same day my former projection-ist co-worker (okay, supervisor), Perch Boy, left to go to some trade school in Kansas. In his absence I became senior projectionist at the 'Plex. I began work the night I got home from San Diego. With my additional quarter raise, I was the five-dollar-an-hour man. Donna Hawkins, the manager of the theater, presented me with an alarm key. I had arrived.

I slept until noon after my first shift as chief moron. As the "in charge" person, my night had been extended by half an hour while inventory was completed and the registers were counted out. Dub was killing the days before school started on one of her too-frequent stays with her aunt and cousins in Shreveport. Having nothing else to do, I called Doug.

"Yeah." It was traditional Doug phone etiquette.

"Hey, I'm back in town. What's up?"

"Who is this?" Doug asked. I was sure he was, as they say in mob movies, bustin' my balls.

"You know who this is."

Doug spoke, but he had moved the phone away from his mouth. He was talking to someone else in his room. He conspicuously forgot to cover the receiver with his hand. "It's somebody who won't tell me who he is," Doug told the other person in the room. "I think it may be P. W." I was pretty sure the second letter stood for *whipped*.

"But I thought you said he was dead." The second voice was Veg's.

"Yeah, but I heard a rumor that he was in town this summer. Someone said they saw him here, but I figured it was just like one of those Elvis sightings." He spoke directly into the phone. "What's it like, you know"—he let his voice quiver—"on the other side?"

"Kiss my ass," I said before hanging up.

Houston, Junior Year

GOD was dead.

And none of us had the energy to revive it. The Grippe hired itself a new guitarist, a sophomore named Ogden. Doug was more interested in appearing in the *Houston Press*, the city's weekly arts and entertainment bible, than the yearbook. No one else had the dynamism to found a new club. Regrettably, I couldn't quite avoid seeing our former leader. He was, along with Dub, one of my fellow thirteen students in Mr. Waters' creative writing class.

And what a strange class it was. On the first day of school, Waters had us all take out some scratch paper. On it, we were to write down a word that we thought described ourselves. Dub scribbled away almost immediately, while I sat there with an eraser in my mouth until he came around to pick up the modest assignment. From that day on, the man referred to us only by the words we'd chosen. I think Dub was initially embarrassed by her selection of "Irresistible." Her shame faded upon learning Doug had christened himself "Stallion." I was known as "Cynic."

Waters issued each of us copies of James Joyce's *Dubliners*. He instructed us to read some of the stories before our next meeting.

"Which ones?" Andy cum Success asked, pen poised.

"Any of them. Any that catch your attention," Sky responded.

Success smirked. "Which ones will we be tested on?" But Sky ignored the question.

"Your homework for tonight—'What I Did This Summer.'"

The class groaned. So much for contemporary approaches to education. I had done this assignment since fifth grade.

"It can't be any longer than one sentence," Sky continued. "Just give me the essence. Spare me the details."

The next day, he had us read them out loud.

In a cold place, devoid of light, I searched for understanding and love.—Goldfish

After a leadership conference in May, I attended a band camp where I won two performance ribbons before heading off to Mock Congress in Austin. (This assignment isn't fair. It needs to be longer.)—Success

During my parents' third honeymoon—a two-month Baltic cruise—I lived with my aunt and uncle and managed not to mutilate my total brat cousins.—Driver

The murky, moss-bottomed home to tadpoles cooled my two feet, and in the pure delight of sunbeam collecting, I scarcely heard the steel-toed boots of impending fall.—Writer

I watched the soaps . . . MTV during the commercials.—Tredder

I joined a Houston boys' club and tried to get out of Clear Lake as much as possible before I found myself playing croquet, eating angel hair pasta with walnut-ajilla chili pesto, and punching Dad's new friends who say what a nice boy I am.—Black and Proud

I answered phones at the Houston Rape Crisis Center.—Medea

Nothing worth writing about.—Rocker

My parents took my little brother and me to Germany, but it wasn't much fun because my dad made us tour Dachau which is where my great-aunt and uncle were killed.—Fat

The highlight of my summer was when Sanders Lownwright got beaned in the back of the head by a foul ball and lost a tooth when his head snapped forward into my cash register while I was handing him a snow cone at the Kiwanis Park concession booth, which only shows how pathetic my life is.—Confused

I pissed off my parents in the following ways: I didn't visit any colleges, I spray-painted the name of my band on my jeep, I refused their $250 offer to cut my hair.—Stallion

I became a woman.—Irresistible

This summer I came to the conclusion that Texas isn't as bad as say, Oklahoma.—Cynic

Or at least that's as close as I can remember. When Dub recited hers, everyone turned and stared at me. Doug sneered. Waters gave a Mr. Spock raised eyebrow of acknowledgment, the kind that withheld judgment.

• • •

I drank as fast I could—four beers into downtown Houston while Dub drove. By the time Missy, Rhonda, Dub, and I arrived at Zelda's for The Grippe's (Mach II) debut, I was in a goofy zone. You know, almost like I wanted to dance. I had a little shoulder shimmy happening by the time this monolithic bouncer painted an impressive black X on the back of my hand with a Marks-A-Lot.

The band tuned and primped onstage. The girls insisted we say hello before they began. I was saddened, but not surprised, to find Doug would be performing shirtless. He looked distracted when we approached.

"You guys are going to be great tonight," Missy assured Doug.

"Good house," was his non sequitur reply.

Good house? I had to cough to prevent flying into hysterics. "Break a leg," I said.

"Yeah," he answered, not looking at me.

I led the girls out of the probable moshing zone and snatched a table when fans of the previous band rushed to escape. Over the next thirty-eight minutes, The Grippe delivered twenty songs ripe with teen angst. They performed with all the fury three boys from Clear Lake can muster. Victims of their haranguing? Neighborhood security patrols. Elderly drivers. Suburban wastelands. I didn't hear my name mentioned in "Fool for Love," but I got edgy anyway. Particular faves included "Scary Mariah Carey" and the caustic "Cineplex Lady"—an obvious tribute to my boss, the only theater manager in town who checked IDs.

Hey Donna, You still wanna?
Cut out the scenes
where the heroine screams
in the sauna?

What they lacked in technical proficiency, they made up for in self-absorption and debauched charm. As much as I didn't want to admit it, Ogden was a better guitar player than Bill. Veg could sing. Once he could play bass, the band might be dangerous. I just wish we had made it out of there before Doug threw his drumsticks into the crowd. It made me physically ill to watch two sophomore girls fight over one of them. My expression left no doubt that I didn't want to wait in the greeting line to pay homage to the conquering heroes.

"Do you think they have a shot?" Rhonda asked me on the car ride home.

"A shot at what?"

"Making it. You know. Of us seeing them on MTV someday."

I thought about Doug playing in an MTV all-star softball game, rounding third and trying to take out Bo Jackson at home plate.

"Oh, I hope so," I said.

We dropped off Rhonda, then Missy. Dub was normally pretty stubborn about keeping her radio tuned to the Rice station no matter how weak the signal became, but as Missy fumbled for her house key, Dub dialed up a classical station.

"I'm tired of loud music," she said.

"Loud something," I said.

Dub pulled out of the driveway. "Sylvia's taking a psychology class at Rice, and she said that their professor told them that, when you're young, you're attracted to someone the opposite of you—personality-wise." I immediately thought of my parents. "But as you get older, you become more attracted to people who are like yourself." Dub blew her bangs out of her eyes. "In the end, either type or relationship has about an equal chance of making it, which is, these days, about zip. So, which type of relationship do you think we have?"

"I think we're alike."

"See, I knew you were going to say that. I think it's obvious we're completely different."

"No, we're not," I said defensively. "We think the same things are cool. We think the same things are fake and stupid. We like the same bands."

"Yeah, but none of that stuff is what counts. It's how you deal with shit, what your first impulse is, that determines your personality—not whether you think country music sucks. You—when you get upset, what do you do? You shut up. Me? I yell. You sit in the back of every classroom and try to hide how smart you are. I make sure everyone knows how brilliant I am. I see everything as gray. You see everything in black and white. We've got everything in common, but we're not at all alike."

"Is that bad?"

"Of course not, sweetie." She patted my knee. We listened to a whole opus . . . or movement . . . or concerto—whatever the hell they call the span of classical music between the whisperings of zombie DJs—before Dub spoke again. "Do you have any of those condoms left?"

"No, me and my other girlfriends, we've been going at it like porn stars."

"That's too bad."

"I might have one left."

Dub took the familiar turn that led to Cottontail Circle, an undeveloped cul de sac accoutered with driveways but as yet no houses or streetlights. We climbed into the backseat of her Civic—and in case anybody asks you, it is possible. Unlike our first time, we weren't so concerned with the poetry of the moment. Only necessary clothes were removed, and those were tossed carelessly aside. I didn't think so much, but it struck me: I was enjoying the moment. From some of the crazy faces Dub was making, I'd say she was too.

●●●

Adapting to Mr. Waters's methods wasn't easy. First of all, we didn't have desks, and with the chairs arranged in a circle, there was no back of the classroom where I could hide. He would ask us what we thought of a story. None of us knew the correct answer, so no one spoke. He had to wring responses from us.

"Tell us what you liked about *Lolita*, Goldfish," or "Medea, how do you think the male characters came across in *The Color Purple*?"

We didn't really have a lively debate until Black and Proud insisted to the class that no white person in the world should have directed *The Color Purple*, an assertion to which several in the class took exception (including Dub, who maintained any woman, black or white, would have been more qualified than any man). The debate was heated. People spoke at the same time. Voices were raised. Class time disappeared. But Sky didn't stop us, nor did he jump in on a side. To him, this was education. It took some getting used to, all this talking, all this contending and justifying in class, having a teacher who eggs us on, tells us to join the fray, to take sides. On this day, it was boys against girls. The subject was James Joyce's *Dubliners*. The girls liked the short story "Eveline." The boys, "Araby."

"Sky." Dub had been the first among us to risk calling him by his much-publicized nickname. He didn't even flinch. He acted like it was normal to call a teacher by something other than Mr. or Mrs. "What is it about 'Araby' that guys like? I mean, it's okay, but nothing happens. A boy goes to the store and decides not to buy a gift for a girl he thought he liked. 'Eveline' is tragic. She sacrifices love for her family."

Sky stretched his legs. His moccasined feet wound up in the middle of the circle. "What is it about 'Araby' that boys like? I can only tell you why I like it." Without looking at his book, he quoted. " 'My body was like a harp and her words and gestures were like fingers running upon the wires.' "

Several of us nodded—that *was* it. And how strange that he should say he could only say what he liked about it. All of us had, in our ten or eleven years of schooling, been taught not to think or offer our opinions. The answers were there in the teacher's guide; our job was to memorize. After a few weeks, most of us adapted to Sky's techniques.

The books Sky assigned I read in my other classes, in the projection booth at the 'Plex, on the Varner couch with Dub doing the same next to me. I was even beating the astronaut to the breakfast table. I would be reading over a bowl of Trix when he marched down the stairs.

Grace's homecoming festivities came and went without any involvement from the former dadaists. Watching other groups working on floats in the parking lot, I caught myself missing the Whiteside barn. *Don't be stupid*, I told myself. *I have Dub now.* The two of us skipped the homecoming dance, but we celebrated our one-year anniversary by ditching school and driving to Lake Charles, Louisiana. Dub's aunt owned a cabin there, and Dub knew where the key was hidden. Dub insisted on going to school early and dropping off the paragraphs Sky had assigned. We were supposed to convince him of the significance of our favorite childhood toy.

"Thanks for getting this to me. You have a safe trip. Oh, and congratulations. A year . . . that's long by high school standards." I didn't figure he would try to stop us, but I was still impressed. Once, Writer had raised her hand and asked to go to the bathroom. Sky had said, "Who am I to stand in the way of Mother Nature?" From then on we just walked out of class whenever we needed to go. No one abused the freedom.

The drive to Lake Charles took three hours. We sang along to the *Saturday Night Fever* eight track Dub got me as an anniversary present. For the next two weeks we used the word *jive* unrepentantly and laughed at our inside joke. The cabin was more your garden variety, small-frame house than the rustic, likely-to-feature-taxidermy, gigantic-fireplace, and bear-rug sort. Still, it was right on the lake and there was no one else around. We made love four times that day. We pretended to be unhappily married to clueless spouses. The cabin was where we carried out our affair. Our pillow talk was the stuff of TV fiction.

"I'd leave him, but I couldn't do that to the kids," Dub said.

"I knew the day I hired you as my secretary that one day you would be mine."

"But what you didn't know was that I would move up the company so fast and you would end up working for me." She pinned me. "Now perform before I fire you on a whim."

Later I returned to the El C and grabbed Dub's anniversary present out of the glove box.

"Whatisit? Whatisit? Whatisit?" Dub said, rubbing her palms together. "Gimme."

She ripped the purple foil wrapping off the small box and lifted its lid.

"Oh, my god, baby, I can't believe this."

Inside were two pearl earrings. I had spent nearly six hundred dollars on them—all the money I saved during the summer. Dub's expression wasn't what I had counted on, though. Her poofy lips curled downward and her brows furrowed. It wasn't a so-happy-you're-sad expression. It was vanilla sad.

"Steve, you need to take these back. This is too much. I mean . . . we're just kids. This is the kind of gift people give on their tenth wedding anniversary." She sympathetically handed the box back to me.

I was too embarrassed to return the earrings. Let's face it. Returning jewelry must be almost as humiliating as actually having it refused. What are you going to say: "They weren't her size" or "She loved me too much to take them"? One day she would accept the gift.

The earrings remained in my glove box. Everything was status quo with Dub; she just didn't want me spending all that money on her. She said she didn't need me to show her I loved her that way. There were other, more pleasurable, ways of expressing our love. We were experimenting with those regularly. We had a routine down in which I said good night, drove down the block, parked the car, and returned on foot to the doors of her bedroom. We'd set the alarm clock for the middle of the night, make love, and fall asleep in each other's arms. The risks involved made me a wreck, but it was worth it.

It was on a morning after one of my late night sallies that I was awakened by the phone ringing.

"Is Alan York there?" asked the voice, obviously military, on the other end.

I thought about it. Normally he was gone by this time, but I hadn't been awakened by the garage door opener like usual.

"Let me check," I said.

"He's supposed to be in a meeting right now." The speaker was irritated.

I stumbled out into the hall in my underwear and approached the astronaut's door. I knocked a couple times, then opened it, yelling, "Telephone." Instead of finding the crisply made bed I expected, I learned, unexpectedly, the old man had a libido. All I saw were four frantic arms reaching for whatever they could find, then a sheet flying up over blond hair.

"Steve. Close the door," the astronaut commanded, but I was already well into that action.

I tried unsuccessfully to go back to sleep. I wanted to call Dub and share the Miracle of Briar Cove with her, but she probably wasn't awake yet.

I mulled over how embarrassed I'd been standing in that doorway. The more I thought about it, the more I resented the fact that I was the one who was rattled. Apparently it wasn't inappropriate for the astronaut to have female company upstairs. I put on some gym shorts, grabbed my *Slaughterhouse Five*, and bounced downstairs. I was buttering toast and pretending to read when the astronaut entered the kitchen. I looked up from the book.

"I'd like to meet your little girlfriend sometime," I said.

"Her name is Miss Darby, and you'll probably meet her in a few minutes if you continue to sit there grinning."

"I think it's great that you're starting to take an interest in girls."

The astronaut didn't have the time to stay and beat me—his meeting must have been terribly important—so I continued eating and listened to the sounds coming from upstairs. Miss Darby looked appropriately shamed when she eventually tiptoed down.

"Muffin?" I asked, holding up a bran one. I was required by all that teenagers hold dear to milk this.

"No . . . thank you, though," she said. "This is pretty awkward." I wasn't helping her. I widened my eyes, but said nothing. "We haven't been introduced. My name is Jacqueline. Jacqueline Darby. You must be Steve."

"Uh-huh."

She remained standing, and I didn't offer her a place to sit. She rocked back and forth from her heels to her toes. Like Mom, she was blond, and I had to admit, pretty. She was young, maybe mid-thirties. Figures. I returned my attention to my book.

"Oh, you're reading Vonnegut. God, I loved Vonnegut. I think I read *Slaughterhouse Five* when I was about your age," Jacqueline said.

"Not too long ago, then?" I said without looking up.

Long pause. "So, you're not going to make this any easier. That's okay. Can I at least use the phone?"

I pointed to the one on the wall. She walked over to it, and I listened as she asked for the number for the Checker Cab Company.

"Look, I can give you a ride somewhere. You don't need to call a cab."

"Are you sure? I don't mind."

I told her I was sure, and ran to throw on some jeans. I didn't have time to shower, so I just tied on a doo rag. I looked my pirate worst. Jacqueline lived on the Clear Lake side of Houston, which was a good thing because I was facing rush hour traffic into the city.

"Your father says you're very bright."

So that was his spin control. *The boy wears earrings, dresses like a bum, can't catch a football, has a freak girlfriend . . . but he's sharp as a tack!* "How did the two of you meet?" I asked once we were on our way.

"My brother introduced us. He works with Alan."

"I figured you met at his health club, or something."

"Well, he certainly is in shape," she volleyed. I guess I deserved it. She thumbed through my eight-track box. "I didn't know anybody still had a machine that played these. God, I think I owned about half of these on eight track. Maybe we *are* about the same age."

"There are more in the glove box, if you want to pick one out," I said, interested in seeing what she would choose.

She pulled Neil Young's *Rust Never Sleeps* out of the glove box, and when she did, a wrapped condom came fluttering out behind it, touching down on Jacqueline's lap.

"Alan said you had a serious girlfriend," she said, stuffing the prophylactic back in the glove box.

Now I was the one who was embarrassed.

•••

For weeks I braced for a summoning into the astronaut's study for a sex lecture. It would have been a short one: don't. When it didn't happen, I knew I owed Jackie big. The astronaut hadn't just blown this one off. If he had been apprised of the flying condom, I would have heard about it. As for Jacqueline, she was becoming a more permanent fixture around *mi casa* than me. As far as I could tell, Jacqueline wasn't spending the night anymore. This got me wondering. I mean, when do adults do it? Dating with a teenager in the house must suck. I posted my work schedule on the refrigerator, just to show the astronaut I cared—or rather, I knew.

Dub asked me about it on the phone.

"Can you imagine your father, you know, in the throes of passion?"

"It's hard for me to imagine the man without a tie."

"Did you ever walk in on your mom and dad when you were little?"

"No. I know everyone else did. Or they heard their mom screaming and thought their dad was hurting her, or something. It's supposed to screw some kids up for years. But my parents had separate bedrooms as far back as I can remember. Jesus, the other day he came into my room and asked me if he looked okay."

"What did you say?"

"I gave him the I'll-say-yes-to-get-you-out-of-my-room yes."

"Good call."

"What other choice did I have?"

●●●

Doug—pardon me—*Stallion* was wearing sunglasses in Sky's classroom, this after I had seen three or four freshmen that day wearing clenched-fist-logoed Grippe T-shirts. A pair of drumsticks emerged conspicuously out of his leather saddlebag, as if to say, worship me. There had been talk, repeated by Dub of all people, that SunDial Records, a Houston independent label, might be interested in signing the band. I could say with absolute certainty that Doug himself had started that rumor. Today he was fanning the fire by replacing his John Deere cap with a SunDial one.

Today's classroom battle centered on Sinéad O'Connor's shredding of the Pope's photo on *Saturday Night Live*. Three camps formed: Dub and Doug's argued that freedom of speech meant she could tear up anyone's photo, and that, furthermore, those who criticized her were fascists; Success, along with Black and Proud, asserted, mainly, that she was a bitch; my camp, which was limited in its membership to me, felt Sinéad was a prima donna for whimpering after catching all the heat. Sure, she had the right to tear up the photo, just as every viewer in Kansas had the right to call her a pretentious, grandstanding, calculating, misinformed moron.

Mere school bells couldn't stop the class from wrestling with the intricacies of the first amendment, but Sky blew his whistle sharply and made a time-out sign with his hands.

"Get out of here!" he shouted whimsically. "Cynic, can I see you after class?"

When the rest of the class was gone, Sky sat on his desk. Though his knees hinged at the edge, his feet reached the ground.

"I wanted to ask your permission to enter one of your essays in a writing contest the Houston Chronicle is sponsoring for high school and college students," he said, scratching his goatee and looking at my paper in his hands.

"Is it good?" I asked.

"One of the best I've ever had the pleasure of reading."

"Yeah, go ahead, then. They won't print it, will they?"

"Only if you win."

I thought about it for a minute. "That's fine. Oh, and thanks." Then I ran out of the room to catch up with Dub. I caught up with her just outside the cafeteria, still savoring victory with Mr. Sunglasses.

"Hey, guess what," I said elatedly.

"What?" Dub said. Doug continued walking.

"Sky wants to enter my story—the one about my

Little League days—in this contest the *Houston Chronicle* is having."

"Baby, that's great. I told you it was good." She hugged me. "Did he say anything about any of the others? Was he going to enter anyone else's?"

"Uh, he didn't say."

Dub looked downcast. I had forgotten how long she had worked on her essay. She had even typed it, though she can't type. I couldn't come over for two nights in a row while she worked. In fact, I even dined at home with Al and Jackie one of those evenings. Dub sighed. I told myself to start being more sensitive to other people's feelings.

• • •

I see little through the windows of the projection booth, not only because of the distortion the thick glass produces, but because I am little interested in what goes on out there in Usherland. I've got too much to worry about, what with films starting every ten minutes, up here on my own. So it was surprising that I spotted the fairly nondescript backside of the astronaut. It wasn't him, so much, that I recognized, as it was his walk: his mastery of locomotive efficiency. Not a wasted twitch in that thirty-six-inch stride. Jacqueline was with him. The astronaut carried both drinks and the tub of popcorn, ungreased, I'm sure. Such a gentleman.

Outside of televised sports, I had never known the astronaut to sit still for passive entertainment. Mom had taken Sarah and me to plays and movies. She had watched Saturday morning cartoons with us, slurping sugary cereal in front of the television right beside us. The astronaut must be pretty interested in Jackie. Who else had gotten him to stray, even for a couple hours, from the Protestant work ethic? I had just started the previews when the two of them entered. I carefully monitored their progress to see if the astronaut had any moves, but in doing so, I neglected my duties. The jeers and shouts of "focus" surprised and unnerved me. I made some quick adjustments, then peeked at the couple below. They hadn't turned around, but I'm sure the astronaut knew it was me bungling this up. He had once said I could screw up a steel ball. I took ironic pride in that.

I hadn't been happy about working this night, anyway. Pseudo-SunDial recording artists, The Grippe, were playing the Vatican, and Dub, Missy, and Rhonda were going. I didn't mind missing the band, but Dub was in jeopardy of becoming a fan. I wanted to be sitting next to her to make sardonic comments throughout the show, to repeat especially insipid lyrics to her.

Plus, Doug had lobbied all week for Sky to come out for the show. That would be a blast. Sky, I was sure, would reach similar conclusions regarding the artistic merits of The Grippe.

◆ ◆ ◆

Had there been a window in Sky's classroomette, I would have stared out of it. Sky was in the middle of one of his few lectures: this one stressing a reliance on hardy nouns and verbs over clunky adjectives and adverbs. I didn't jump in when he asked us to replace the weak verb/adverb combination "walked slowly" with a single descriptive verb. My enthusiastic classmates offered "plodded," "slogged," "trudged," "limped," "ambled," "strutted," "sauntered," "strolled," "wandered." I kept "moseyed" to myself. I wasn't uninterested in the lecture, just distracted. Sarah was arriving later that evening for the Thanksgiving holidays. After we picked her up, she, Dub, and I were going straight to a Rice party. I was concurrently excited about seeing Sarah and nervous about taking her to a college party. Sarah might think like an adult, but she still looked no older than her fifteen years.

I continued to let Sky's light southern drawl wash over me. Though I had lived most of my life in the South, I still equated the dialect with either A) stupidity, or B) dishonesty. But in Sky's case, I sensed a roots-consciousness, a southern heritage, a William Faulkner nobility. I barely caught the words, ". . . has named Steve York their top high school creative writer."

I felt Dub's arms wrap around me. The rest of the class, including Doug, clapped. One of their own had succeeded. Sky stood and walked across the circle. He handed me an embossed certificate that featured the *Houston Chronicle*'s mod, sans serif masthead across the top. My name, Steven Richard York, was engraved in calligraphic script below. Sky shook my hand.

"They're having an awards luncheon next Friday, very coat and tie. They expect you and your father to attend," Sky said.

After class I waited for everyone but Sky to clear out.

"Sky, I was wondering if maybe you could go to the banquet with me?"

"What about your father?"

"NASA's sending him out of town next week," I lied.

Sky looked at me for a moment, and I was afraid I was snagged. "I think they'll give me a sub for this. Yeah, we can go."

"Thanks," I said and ran off to catch Dub.

San Diego, Senior Year

The prettiest waitress at Cap's, the one who looks like Patricia Arquette, mistook me for some guy named Corliss from her poli-sci class at UCSD. She sat down with me in the booth and asked me about the German parliament before realizing her mistake.

"God, I'm sorry. You look just like him."

"I wish I could help," I said sincerely.

"I wish you could too. What *is* your major?"

I took a long, black, grimaceless sip. "Psychology." Could I have said anything further from the truth? I've never correctly divined anyone's thoughts in my life.

"Well, maybe I'll see you around campus." She stood up and nodded yes to some unspoken question, then stuffed her fists into the coffee-stained pockets of her apron before leaving. She turned to serve a neighboring booth. I noticed the flawless lines created by her snug jeans. I remembered Doug writing me about art classes in college that hired students to model nude. Is there anyone on planet Earth more ready to be out of high school?

Houston, junior year

The astronaut insisted on picking up Sarah from the airport; it was an errand neither of us would bow out of. He whistled along to the Muzak he located on the Lincoln's radio. Our conversation on the way to the airport was limited.

"How's school?"

"Fine," I said.

"How's work?"

"Fine," I said.

Sarah's plane was delayed for twenty minutes, so the astronaut and I each grabbed a section of a *Chronicle* that had been left on a row of seats. We read without speaking for the duration: he the news, me the entertainment. We stood as the plane pulled into the gate. Sarah was one of the last off, but when she spotted us, she weaved through the lame, infant, and elderly between us. She gave the astronaut a huge hug, and he hugged her back with at least equal affection. The two yammered on and on for the entire trip back to the house. I grabbed Sarah's bags out of the trunk.

"Pick a guest room . . . any guest room," I said.

"I'll take what's behind door number three," she said. I lugged her bags up the stairs.

When I came back down, I glimpsed that mysterious expression on the astronaut's face again. It looked something like a smile. Yep, definitely at least a cousin of a smile. Corners of the mouth turned up. Eyebrows slightly raised in amusement. He lost points for showing zero teeth. His lips were, in fact, vacuum sealed. For him, though, it was as close as one got.

Sarah and I left an hour later to pick up Dub for the party at Rice.

"You sure seem to make the old man happy."

"So do you. You just can't tell."

Right.

● ● ●

The most embarrassing part of the awards luncheon was when they read my essay out loud. Sky hadn't warned me that they would do it, so imagine my shock when the editor in chief of the *Houston Chronicle* took out her reading glasses and unfolded the lavender typing paper Dub had lent me.

LAZY HAZY DAZE
BY STEVE YORK

I was obliged at ten to go somewhere I'd never been; a soldier venturing to unknown lands to fulfill his American duty. And I was prepared, armed with a deadly dose of bubble gum and a Mike Schmidt autographed mitt. A boy pulled from the ranks of sandlot ball and trading cards finally getting his shot in the bigs.

It was a steamy day at the Cocoa Beach Little League fields. The sun's rays, interrupted only by dragonflies, blanketed the well-tended green that surrounded the dirt diamond, and I stood forefront in the line of other boys my age being sized and tested for talent in baseball's cattle auction.

I wasn't much to look at, actually: a skinny, no-shouldered kid possessing the reflexive speed of a traffic jam, with baseball fundamentals that would have landed me a second-string position on a girls' softball squad.

Or, as it happened, a one-way ticket to right field.

Outfield in Little League is a camp out, a resting place for those who never needed a rest. We were the guys who stared down the three strikes and sat back on the bench aimlessly, always wondering how we underestimated the ball's velocity, though the thing usually crept by at no more than forty-five miles per hour. We were a common breed in the league, but at least I was finely woven into the American fabric.

I was taken in that year by a Giants club who either felt sympathetic or whose prior successes had earned them the last pick. Either way, weeks into my rookie season, I had taken a firm position in the dugout, then eventually staked out my territory near the advertisements that made up the back fence.

So this is what it was all about—the red, white, and blue, apple pie and a cloudless spring afternoon spent enjoying hot dogs and a Coke at the ballpark.

And it was happening all over America. I had

become one with the freshly-mowed-lawn-and-
whatever-was-cooking-at-the-concession-stand
scent. It seemed a bit too trivial to worry about
the game or chant "batter, batter, batter." This
was it; all I needed was to stand out among the
weeds of left field and stare up at the bright sta-
dium lights that watched over me and told everyone that I existed.

There were players there with the natural
swing of Will Clark or the infield wizardry of Ozzie
Smith. Players you had no doubt in ten years
would wind up on the NBC Game of the Week.
They were cut from that just-a-little-pinch-
between-your-cheek-and-gum mold. The kind who
would judge a bat on its size and weight, instead
of just picking one up and swinging.

I, on the other hand, suited in a jersey that
drooped out in all directions, picked up a bat and
basked in the limelight for the time it took for
three more strikes.

Which was long enough to be entwined in
the American dream.

Apparently my experience had some universality to it.
The assembled civic leaders and reporters responded
warmly when the reader concluded by exhaling and placing a hand over her heart.

Sky leaned into me and whispered, "If you're not
careful, boy, you're going to lose your iconoclast membership card."

I smirked and whispered back, "Keep clapping, fools.
One day all this will be mine!"

The college winner, Isshee Ayam, came from the
University of Houston. Her essay, "Reflections of a
Statistic," about growing up in the Fifth Ward, made mine

sound like pinheaded high school drivel. Afterward, Sky convinced her to come speak to our class.

"But if this is any example of the work your students are doing, I don't know if I could teach them anything," she said, nodding at me and making me blush.

"No, Steve's a special case. And I think even his highness could learn a few things from you."

I'm afraid I glowed on the trip back to Grace. Maybe there was something I could do well. Then I thought again of Isshee's paper.

"Do you learn to write that much better in college?" I asked Sky.

"It's not so much learning as it is living. You can improve your technique through classes and through reading, but you've got to have some truth to put behind the language. Otherwise, no one will connect to it. It's tough, for example, to write about love until you've had your heart broken."

The next morning I read *Breakfast at Tiffany's* at the breakfast table for twenty minutes before I noticed, hanging by a Texas Credit Union magnet on the refrigerator, an article clipped from the *Houston Chronicle* about yours truly. The headline read, UH, GRACE STUDENTS WIN *CHRONICLE* WRITING CONTEST. I got up and pulled off the Post-it note on which the astronaut had scribbled, "Good job!" Two photos dominated the layout: one of Isshee Ayam and her mother and one of Sky and me. I scanned the article; there was no mention of the astronaut. I guess they hadn't figured that one out. My essay had been reprinted in its entirety.

I couldn't find Dub when I got to school. She wasn't in our regular before-school cafeteria spot as far away from the Amy Grant–stocked jukebox as possible. I checked the Joshua Tree, though it was getting too cold to hang out outside. No luck. On a whim I investigated

Sky's classroom. Bingo. She was hunched up over his desk looking down at a paper. Sky was pointing at a spot on the page and appeared to be explaining something.

"Hey, Dub. I couldn't find you anywhere this morning," I said, getting her attention. I swear I said it without any attitude.

"Well, it's not like we're connected at the hip, you know. We *are* capable of going places without each other."

"Oh, I'm sorry . . . I didn't mean to—"

"Forget it," she said.

Houston, Christmas Vacation, Junior Year

Sky had a Christmas party at his house the day we got out for Christmas vacation. The invitations he handed out a week earlier were handmade in kindergarten fashion: red and green construction paper cut into Christmassy bells and angels, ample Elmer's and glitter applied. On each he had attached a pink-cheeked St. Nick gift label, the kind that identify the giver and receiver. In lieu, he had written a quote for each of us on the label. Mine read, *"I talk and talk and talk, and I haven't taught people in fifty years what my father taught me by example in one week.—Mario Cuomo."* Below that, he had written, "These are your Santa clauses—my yuletide gifts of wisdom." Sky had a pretty sixth-grade sense of humor sometimes.

I offered to show Dub mine, but she said they were personal messages from Sky and that we ought to keep them to ourselves out of respect for him. I looked around the circle. Our classmates were passing their invitations around, reading their consecrated messages to one another. Fine. We'll be the faithful disciples. The invitation also included a map to Sky's house.

• • •

Sky couldn't afford to live in Clear Lake on his teacher's salary. His gabled house would have been an anachronism among the tracts of familiar conventionality of Clear Lake homes, anyway. Located a few miles outside the coastal side of the 'burb, it had a screen door. It had hardwood floors. Windows were raised and lowered with ropes, weights, and pulleys.

Sky had an ice chest full of soft drinks. He also had a giant thermos full of hot, rum-free eggnog. Under the tree I saw the baker's dozen gifts, without a doubt earmarked for us students. Sure, Sky taught four other classes of students, but those were standard, mandatory English IV classes. Those present had elected to take creative writing from him. He had freedom with us that he didn't elsewhere in a school judged by its achievement test scores.

Doug showed up with a date, some sophomore from Memorial he met at a gig. I thought she was cute in a band chick sort of way. Dub didn't agree.

"He could do a lot better than her. Is she wearing anything that isn't leather? Add a belt to that ensemble and she'll start mooing."

I excused myself to find a bathroom. Sky pointed me in a direction, but the door was locked. I followed the hall to stairs leading up. Spurred on by my full bladder, I took the stairs to a door. Inside was Sky's room. His bed was king sized with darkly stained posts at all four corners. Anyone other than Sky, I noted, would probably need a stepladder to get on it. Unframed modern art hung from all four walls, purple swirls and stick people, pieces that looked like spray-painted sections of the Berlin Wall. On his dresser, between candles of all shapes and sizes, were framed pictures of people I guessed were his family, one of him with what I presumed were two older sisters in front of a Pacer. Another gave me reason to pause. It was a wedding photo, and a clean-shaven Sky was the groom. He'd never told us he'd been married. Come to think of it, he'd never told us much about his life. Sky was a listener, the best listener. He seemed to pick up on everything. He had, earlier in the semester, given us his home phone number in case we "just needed someone to talk to," but any words coming out of his mouth were advice, encouragement. Philosophy—not history. I remembered him referring to a brief teaching stint somewhere in the Southeast, where he was born, before coming to Grace early in his career. That was as much as I knew about him.

I exited down the stairs without finding the bathroom. The music from *A Charlie Brown Christmas* was playing, and Sky was having people gather around the tree for the big gift exchange. He made us each open our presents one by one. Everyone received books, but each of us got a different one. He gave Doug *Hammer of the Gods,* an unauthorized biography of Led Zeppelin. Dub received a D. H. Lawrence book that we had talked about in class during a discussion of banned literature. I was the only one who didn't receive a book; instead I got an envelope. Inside was a receipt for *Anchors Away,* Grace's yearbook.

San Diego / Houston, Christmas Vacation, Junior Year

Something was going wrong, but I had no idea how to stop it. Even if I knew how, I knew it couldn't be done from my mother's house in San Diego. Long distance phone calls between Dub and me had always begun with *I miss yous* and ended with *I love yous.* Now I was always the caller and she always had to run off somewhere.

"Let's take another trip up to your aunt's cabin when I get back. It's probably cold enough now that we could make a fire," I suggested early on Christmas Eve.

Silence. "I'm sorry, what were you saying?"

"I said we should go to your aunt's cabin."

"I don't know if that's a good idea. We're lucky we didn't get caught last time. Hey, I've got to amscray. Missy's here to pick me up."

"On Christmas Eve?"

"Last-minute shopping, Sweetie."

"You know I love—"

"I know you do. Gotta go, bye."

I let four days languish by before giving in and calling again. On Christmas Day, Sarah had to drag me out of bed to open gifts. I meticulously unwrapped boxes of boxer shorts, colognes, and floppy disks. I moaned little thank yous.

"Someone put the Grinch out of his misery," Sarah said between tearing open her own packages.

When I called Dub again on the 29th, I was pissed.

"So were you going to call me, ever, if I didn't call you?"

"Steve, we're not married, you know. Jesus, you freak out over the smallest things. You know we've got relatives over here. It's like a zoo. Cousins getting into all my shit. Sylvia's on my back. And now I've got to deal with you obsessing out in California. Like I didn't have enough headaches."

"So that's what I am, a headache?"

"Oh, Steve, don't do this."

And I hung up on her. I couldn't believe I did it. I ran out to the beach where I could cry as loudly as I wanted, and I couldn't pick up a phone to call her back to apologize.

The next day I asked if I could return to Texas.

"This is my time, honey," my mom said. "I only get you so many weeks a year. It's just a couple of days you're talking about. You can work things out with Dub then."

"Please, Mom," I said desperately. "I'm not going to be any fun around here anyway. I'll convince the astronaut to give you a couple extra days somewhere down the line." My voice was cracking and my eyes were unrehearsed watery. "Just let me change my ticket."

"He's your father. I wish you would call him that."

"Whatever."

"Oh, baby, it's going to be all right."

I arrived home sixteen hours later. It was nearly midnight. I called Dub's house from the airport. Maureen answered groggily.

"Steve, she's spending the night over at Missy's."

I sped down I-45 toward Missy's. I caught a glimpse of myself in the rearview mirror. I looked insane. The dark circles around my eyes aged me by a decade. My skin was clammy, and I was shaking. My heart felt like a hummingbird's. If I didn't see Dub tonight I was sure I would die.

The light in Missy's room was on when I pulled up in front of her house. I ran through the side gate and pounded on her window, calling my girlfriend's name. Missy appeared and slid the window open.

"Steve! What the hell are you doing? Are you crazy? You're going to wake up my parents!"

I felt myself crying in front of Missy, but I didn't care. "Where's Dub? I need to see Dub."

"I don't know where she is, Steve. Why don't you go home tonight. Find her tomorrow." She looked at me, and I saw the pity. "Wait there. I'm coming outside." But by the time she made it to her door, I was squealing off down the street to Doug's.

I should have seen it coming. All her bullshit about opposites attracting. The way the two of them fought. The way Doug treated me after I started going out with

Dub. Dub making fun of Doug's date. Getting dragged to all his shows. I wasn't aware of any of the streets or turns or stoplights as I drove. When I found myself on Doug's street, I thought my heart would explode. I could hear it beating. I just knew it was going to erupt out of my chest like in *Alien* and devour me. Finding neither Dub's nor Doug's car in front of the house only amplified the ache. They could be anywhere, and I had nowhere to start looking. I put my head on the steering wheel and began bawling between screams of "Why?" That's all I could think of to say, "Why?"

I wanted to cry on my best friend's shoulder, but my only friend was Dub. I began driving aimlessly. I attempted to force rational thought to re-enter my mind. Just because neither Dub nor Doug were around, it didn't mean they were together. Or if they were together, it didn't mean they were *together* together. Mrs. Varner could have mistakenly said Missy instead of Sylvia or Rhonda. And Doug—who knew where he was at one in the morning? Who cared?

Strangely, I thought of Sky. He said he would always be there if we needed to talk. I didn't know if that meant we could drop in uninvited in the middle of the night to spill our guts, but I couldn't think of anything else to do. I started feeling better as I made my way out of the city limits to my teacher's house. I couldn't believe I was doing it.

When I first saw it, I was momentarily relieved. Dub's Civic was sitting in the driveway in front of Sky's house. She wasn't with Doug. But what was she doing here? Did she need to talk to Sky, also? In the middle of the night? About me, maybe? I parked in the road. But why weren't the lights on? There was a glimmer, and it came from the window I figured to be Sky's bedroom.

The light came from candles.

This time I didn't cry. I stared at the irregular rhythm of shadows against the curtains. I imagined shrinking, crawling under the windowpane, and watching unnoticed from the ledge. Seeing Dub make those faces that I thought only I would see. Was Sky calling her "Irresistible" in that ocean of a bed? I kept thinking that if she left in the next ten minutes, everything would be fine. But she didn't leave, and I'd give her another ten. I tore open my glove box, hoping to find something sharp. I wanted to hurt myself. Cut my throat with a screwdriver. Drink a can of STP. All I could find was a pair of pearl earrings.

At dawn I staggered like a drunk to Dub's car and left the small box under her windshield wiper.

Houston, junior Year

I quit going to creative writing. No one in the attendance office caught on, as Sky never checked roll. I volunteered for every shift available at the 'Plex and worked every night. I knew Dub's class schedule. Avoiding her was easy enough, though in an unscheduled trip to the parking lot in April, we almost bumped into each other. For the second and final time, I saw her stammer. I walked away without speaking.

During spring break, with most of Grace's students elsewhere, Ronnie, a twenty-three-year-old who I supervised at work, turned me on to getting high. I got fired two weeks later when Donna busted me for smoking in the projection booth. My grades turned to shit, but my previous averages saved me from failing anything but English. I left Houston immediately after my last final, driving nonstop to San Diego.

It didn't take me long to find people who shared my newest hobby.

San Diego, Senior Year

Summer is here. Though today is the last day of classes, teachers stopped teaching weeks ago. Students stopped learning months earlier. Oddly, I've been one of the score of seniors still showing up regularly to classes. I've wagered a "Night of Infinite Pleasures" with Allison that I can make straight A's during the final grading period without her help. I'm not worried so much about not being able to keep up if I miss a class; I'm afraid ditching would remind teachers of my earlier sporadic-at-best attendance. Come grade-giving time, I want them thoroughly enchanted by my bushy-tailedness.

I printed out the final pages of my epic, tentatively titled "Knee Deep in the Heart of Texas," and handed them to DeMouy. I had never stuck around while DeMouy read my prose. Today was different. Today it was over. A herd of gazelle thundered across the Serengeti that was DeMouy's stereo. Elephants trumpeted my impending release. While he read, I brewed myself a cranberry-apple tea. I smuggled the mug out of Cap's weeks ago for this express purpose.

"So that's how you ended up here," DeMouy said after flipping the final page.

"Sad, but true," I said.

We sat there for a moment, but the silence didn't seem uncomfortable. If there was a place I was cozy in this diploma factory, it was this chair. He put his hands behind his head and leaned back in his chair.

"Have you made a final decision about school?"

"I had Mom send in my housing deposit for the University of Washington."

"No beach."

"Yeah, but there's water. And plenty of ships leaving the harbor. All day. All night. They've got great bands, great coffee. They're giving me a shitload of scholarship money." I took a slug of my tea. "Plus, I've got some relatives, distant ones, up there."

"Still interested in that career in counseling?"

"It's taken me four years to get out of high school. I will neither require, nor request, a bathroom pass again in my life." I looked across the desk at DeMouy. "If you could do it all over again, would you still be a counselor?"

"I don't know. I miss the classroom sometimes."

"But you'd go into education again? Man, I don't get it. I watched you at the end of the year assembly. How can you put up with getting no respect from a bunch of seventeen-year-olds? Kids fight in your office. They puke on your shirt."

"Every time I have a bad day, like those you're so kind to remind me of, something happens that turns it around. We get someone into college who didn't think he'd make it. We find scholarship money for someone who needs it. I see kids who should never graduate—because they're getting beaten up at home or because they've got a learning disability or because they get pregnant—make it across that stage."

DeMouy opened the bottom right file drawer of his desk. He pulled out a bulging folder labeled YORK, STEVEN R. I hadn't seen it since my first trip in. From within the folder he pulled out a transcript. He pushed it across the desk. I scanned it and discovered the modification. My failing grade in English had been changed to an A. DeMouy's signature appeared by the new grade.

"Sometimes I get to see sharp kids put their lives back together."

San Diego, Graduation

Toby the Party weaved in and out of the line of soon to be graduates all standing in gowns, awaiting the signal to file into the auditorium for the commencement ceremony. Toby was going to have to take a second crack at his senior year. *There but for the grace of . . . oh, whatever,* I thought, amusing myself.

"You look stoked," I said to Toby when he made it to where Tonya Zapruder and I moored the graduates.

"Jesus, York, where have you been hiding? We better see your ass out tonight. It's party season. There'll be weed, speed, and need out on the beach tonight, boy. What have you been up to lately? Are you really hangin' with that Kimble chick? Tell me it ain't so!"

" 'Fraid so, Tob."

Toby shook his head. "Chicks, man, chicks."

As he spoke, tubas called on us gowned ones to begin our crawl through the visitors' portal. Allison and I were separated by literally hundreds of graduates. She landed a front-row seat by graduating in the top 10 percent of the class. She was probably already seated while I was still considering buying a bag of cherry sours from the candy machine in the gym tunnel. I spotted the family—Cindy, Chuck, Sarah, and Danny—almost immediately upon emerging from the portal. Sarah waved frantically, and I winked at her. I'd received a telegram earlier in the day from the astronaut, saying he would be unable to attend because of a conflict with work. I told Sarah she could have the extra ticket for Danny. I'm sure Danny was elated.

The choir sang and the band played. The principal swelled and our valedictorian urged. The class in question slouched. Finally, it was time for the big walk. I cheered when Allison was called across the stage. I scanned the audience, but I didn't see anyone I guessed to be her father. My contingent, however, helped make up for his absence. A full thirty minutes passed before I had to leave my seat. I tried to open my senses to every vibration, every smell and sound. I attempted to channel relevant images from my past—studying Latin as an eighth grader, typing homework as a freshman, falling in love as a sophomore, throwing away my junior year, trying to put my life back together as a senior. When I came back to reality it was time to climb the steps to the stage. I shook hands with a couple of school board members. They congratulated me. Then I heard my name, *"Steven Richard York."* I discerned Sarah's scream. Allison's wolf whistle from the front row was out of character and perfectly timed. I shook hands with the principal. DeMouy held my diploma at the end of the line.

"Here, you deserve this," he said as he presented the document.

I didn't know how to respond. I shook his hand firmly. I felt like a man. "DeMouy, I . . ." But I couldn't finish. He had to pick up the Zapruder diploma, the last one on the table.

Before Allison and I drove out of the parking lot that night, I wrote a note on the back of a book cover. I left it under the windshield wiper of DeMouy's Plymouth Reliant.

J. D.—You never let me down.—S. Y.
P. S. Boss ride!

San Diego, Summer After Senior Year

Allison left for Cal Berkeley, DeMouy's alma mater, today. They're paying for everything, full ride. It's hard to picture her walking down Telegraph Avenue in her khaki skirt and Top-Siders. Maybe she'll change. I sometimes think she groomed her image here to keep Wakefield at a distance. It worked with everyone but me. We spent a lazy three months together since graduation. By the time she left we were both prepared. We made no promises. We thanked each other verbally and nonverbally. I knew I'd miss her.

She invited me over for dinner one night not too long after she paid off her "Night of Infinite Pleasures" score. It was a sort of a "Well, Dad, here he is . . ." evening. I prepped myself for a fatherly interrogation. I invented possible careers. I memorized league standings from the sports page. I practiced my handshake. I needn't have. Terry Kimble had the grip I would imagine from Marie Antoinette. I spent the salad-to-lasagna lull trying to draw responses from him. All I could get him to talk about was Texas.

"Mom and Dad lived in Beaumont right after they got married," Allison explained.

After a meal every bit as good as one of Mom's and Chuck's all-day-in-the-kitchen affairs, we did dishes as her father fell asleep to *The People's Court.* Wrinkled hand to wrinkled hand, she led me into her father's bedroom. Propped up on his nightstand was a family photograph. Her handsome mother and brother—then a fourteen-year-old—caught my attention first. I grinned at Allison in pigtails, but it was the sight of her father that stunned me. It was hard picturing the man in the photo as the same one snoring on the sofa. The man in the picture was thin, smiling, proud. The clean-shaven patriarch had one hand on his daughter's arm; his opposite shoulder seemed to wrap around the rest of the family. They were safe with him.

"That's how I remember him," Allison said.

As I took Allison to the airport for her flight into San Francisco and the rest of her life, I thought about how lucky her father and I were to have had her in our lives. My time with her was over, though I was sure we would stay in touch. I kept thinking I should be sad, but I felt content more than anything. Now, I'm not saying I won't want to call her every day, and she'll probably die without me, but why ruin something so perfect trying to stay together?

Houston, Summer After Senior Year

Houston was, as I had left it, sweltering and breezeless. I sat in the immense backseat of the Lincoln with my sister. The astronaut, like me, wore a tuxedo. Jacqueline, in a canary chiffon dress, turned to converse with Sarah and me.

"Are you looking forward to your senior year?" she said to my sister. Sarah began a long account of her intentions for the upcoming school year: increasing the number of parking spaces for students, leading the academic bowl team to state, perfecting a countertop cold fusion generator that runs on coffee grounds and Styrofoam packing peanuts. I drifted off when she began. I tried to steel myself for the upcoming horror show. I knew the routine. I would be introduced by the astronaut to countless members of the military and local social glitterati, "Son, you remember Colonel Edmunds, don't you?" Of course, my only encounter with the colonel in question had come when I was in diapers. But I will bear this. I will shake hands and dispense "of courses" like each one didn't chip off a little piece of my soul. I will smile for the photographer from the *Houston Chronicle* society page. I will answer in polite clichés any questions asked of me. Then, with my filial duties complete, I will escape behind some tapestry, a bottle of Dom Perignon in hand, satisfied that I, too, can be a complete fake. I wondered if any former presidents would be at the ceremony.

When the astronaut and I went to pick up the tuxedos earlier in the day, the woman behind the counter handed us each other's rentals. It wasn't until we were standing beside each other in front of the full-length mirror that we noticed the error. He couldn't button his collar and his slacks dragged the ground. In the mirror I noticed I was perhaps a half inch taller than the astronaut.

"My, what handsome men!" our saleslady said.

Looking out the back window I was surprised to see we were leaving Clear Lake and heading into downtown Houston. We pulled into a metered space, and the astronaut asked Jacqueline for quarters. I followed the couple up the steps of the Old Harris County Courthouse building, feeling awfully self-conscious about wearing a tuxedo. I looked at Sarah for a sign, but she just shrugged her shoulders. We passed lines of people paying for traffic tickets, applying for liquor licenses, registering vehicles. We climbed a wide flight of marble stairs with an antique, hand-carved polished banister that indicated this building had once been used for something more important than minor court procedures. The astronaut stopped outside a door on which L. CERVANTES, JUSTICE OF THE PEACE was painted in 1890s gold rush–style lettering.

"We got everybody?" he asked. He didn't need a spoken answer. The four of us were pretty easy to check off. I noticed he was holding Jacqueline's hand. PDA from the astronaut? The apocalypse couldn't be far behind.

Inside, I was introduced to Ben and Dottie Darby, Jacqueline's parents, and Lupe Cervantes, our gregarious and blatantly female justice of the peace. That was it. There were seven of us in the crowded office. I wondered if we would soon leave for a larger hall.

"Let's get started," Ms. Cervantes said, ending my speculation.

The justice of the peace leaned back against her desk. Jacqueline and the astronaut stood in front of her. Dottie flanked her daughter. Sarah and Ben sat in padded chairs—high dollar by city government standards—against the back wall. I stood just behind and to the side of the astronaut. The "service" took all of seven minutes, including my fumbling and subsequent dropping of the ring. I had to get on my hands and knees and fetch it from under Cervantes's desk. Ben belly-laughed and Sarah joined him. I could feel myself turn red. When I finally found the ring, I stood and offered it to the astronaut. I looked him directly in the eye, expecting to see agitation. Instead, he nodded to me reassuringly. I put the ring on his palm.

Ultimately it sunk in: This was *it*—the entire ceremony. There would be no VIPs, no society columnists, no long greeting lines. Why, then, did he care whether I showed, let alone agreed to be his best man? I watched the astronaut as he repeated the vows. His voice was so strong. I had seen weddings where the groom trembled and squeaked each pledge. Not the astronaut. He made it very clear he intended to marry this woman, to love, honor, and obey. He would, too—of this I was certain. The astronaut didn't make promises lightly. I thought of his divorce from Mom. I had wanted to put it out of my head since the night Sarah had tried to enlighten me about the causes. I had spent four comfortable years blaming the astronaut; but, thinking about it, the astronaut would have never gotten a divorce of his own volition. Divorce is failure, and the astronaut simply couldn't stomach failure.

No, something forced his hand. Mom wasn't happy; that was for sure. She knew she was second to his career. She knew she didn't have an equal partnership. I had been right about these things. The astronaut wasn't especially sensitive, tender, romantic. Had that led her to another man? Sarah sure thought so. I didn't like imagining it. If it were true, it would explain a lot of things: why the astronaut didn't fight the divorce, why he didn't show up for my graduation, why he was never around when Mom came to pick up Sarah, why we had moved.

Of course, that had to be it. I thought about having to get away from Houston after everything that happened with Dub and Sky. I couldn't stand to drive the same streets, to walk the same halls, to talk to shared friends, to be around anyone who possibly knew what had happened. I had to leave, and so had the astronaut.

He had known all along who I blamed for their split, for our move, for the separation of Sarah and me. He knew who I would have chosen—and eventually did choose—to live with once I had the option. And he had said nothing. He let me keep thinking of my mother as the heroine and himself the tyrant. That must have killed him, but he said nothing. Now he was putting his life back together. I wasn't here for show. I *was* his best man.

"I now pronounce you husband and wife," Cervantes said. The newlyweds kissed lightly and we clapped.

Cervantes circled around to a dorm-room-sized refrigerator behind her desk and withdrew a bottle of cheap champagne. From a filing cabinet she pulled out seven glasses of assorted sizes and shapes. She popped the cork while everyone hugged Jacqueline and shook the astronaut's hand. Jacqueline escaped her father's embrace and approached me. I looked down and adjusted my cummerbund.

"Hey, handsome," Jacqueline said, "a kiss for the bride?"

"Uh, sure," I answered, hopelessly embarrassed. She offered me her cheek. I tried to pucker, but I'm afraid all she got was the faint pressing of dry lips on the side of her face.

"Thank you," she said, sounding sincere. Then she hugged me. Sarah hugged her next, enthusiastically. How could the two of us be so different? Didn't we have the same basic genetic coding and similar upbringings? Cervantes walked around the room, handing us glasses from a plastic serving tray. The next thing I knew, everyone was looking at me expectantly.

"You're supposed to make the toast, nimrod," Sarah stage-whispered.

"Oh," I said. They should have issued me some sort of best man handbook; I wasn't prepared for this. I recalled the first day I'd met Jacqueline. "To Alan and Jacqueline," I said, raising my Texas sesquicentennial souvenir glass. "May he always forget strategic defense meetings, and may she always be worth it."

Everyone clinked glasses. I touched the astronaut's

last, but before he drank, he saluted me with his glass. I returned the gesture and the two of us sipped our drinks.

Afterward, Dottie took out one of those Fun Shot disposable cameras and had Cervantes take a group picture of the complete wedding party.

I rode shotgun in the Lincoln as we left the courthouse. Jacqueline sat between the astronaut and me. Sarah rode in the backseat with our new stepgrandparents. Before we pulled away from the curb, the astronaut turned in his seat and addressed everyone.

"How does barbecue sound?"

I knew just what he had in mind—the Calvary Baptist Church in Huntsville, a good forty-five minutes north of Houston. He had offered to take me when I lived in Houston, but I had always refused. I had known, after all, that it was his favorite. This time I joined fully in my brisket-lovin' family's enthusiasm.

The cinder block Calvary Baptist Church and Barbecue serves meals "family style." The restaurant occupies an offshoot—probably a garage in a former manifestation—of the congregation hall, and six days a week the men of the church barbecue ribs, brisket, and sausage over hickory pits outside the building while the women prepare the coleslaw, potato salad, sweet tea, and bread that serve as the only sides. Every dish came to our indoor picnic table on heaping unmatched platters. We ate with disposable forks and knives that came sealed in plastic along with our salt, pepper, and napkin. We were the only white people—a crucified Jesus adorning the church events calendar excepted—in the joint. I thought momentarily of the teenaged astronaut as the sole non-Hispanic grape picker in Yakima County.

"They're building a brand-new church across the street to replace this one. They say it's going to be a half-million-dollar affair with stained glass and a pipe organ. Business is that good here," the astronaut said, looking impressed and imbibing more grease in a bite than I had seen him consume in three years' of breakfasts. The man had a vice.

"It seems funny," Sarah said, barbecue sauce dripping down her chin, "that the wedding wasn't in a church, but that the reception is."

"Well, Jacqueline said she wanted a church wedding. This was our compromise." Then I heard the most unfamiliar sound. The astronaut laughed, not one of his suffocated chuckles, but an honest from-the-gut laugh.

◆◆◆

That evening I called Doug. He invited me over, and we sat by his pool in the 95-degree Texas night and talked. He told me about his plans to open up an all-ages music club on the drag in Austin. I told him about this weird dream I'd been having where I was competing for the University of Washington fencing team.

The next morning, I woke to the sound of car doors slamming. I pulled back the shades and went cold. Sarah was getting out of Dub's Civic. Apparently, she had spent the night with her. Dub was already out of the car. Her hair was the original brown color I had seen only in elementary school pictures. It was so long, it nearly reached her waist. Her clothing was standard issue—nothing remained from our former wardrobe of rebellion. She hugged my sister. I watched her huge mouth as it manipulated good-byes. Everything about her was so familiar, but I saw a stranger. All my vital signs stopped in anticipation of the fallout. I quit breathing. My heart paused. My knees prepared to give way.

And then . . . nothing.

The last thing I wanted to do was to run outside and scream at her or take her in my arms or slit my wrists and bleed all over her car. If I felt anything, it was stupid and ashamed. I crawled back under my covers and listened as the Civic door slammed shut and Dub drove away for good.

I contemplated the one item hanging in my room. On the far wall, the photograph Sarah had taken after my freshman year, the one of the lost swan landing on Clear Lake, still hung. I realized then why she chose this particular shot for me. I thought of its twin hanging in the astronaut's study, the one of the panicked salamander, wide-eyed and frightened having just lost half of itself. I knew then, too, why Sarah had framed that one for him.

●●●

I left York Manor the next morning. All I was taking to college were a beaten suitcase stuffed with T-shirts and jeans and the computer I hadn't wanted as an eighth grader.

"I'm leaving," I yelled into the house. I swung my keys around my index finger and walked the short sidewalk to the El Camino.

"Hold on there a minute, Steve. I've got something for you," the astronaut shouted as he jogged from the house, Sarah on his heels. He held an unwrapped box in his outstretched hand. I stopped before getting in my car, and he slid the package across my hood. "One last graduation present."

I severed the Scotch tape with my thumbnail and opened the box. I pulled out a huge sweatshirt.

"Steve, let me see the front," Sarah ordered.

Holding it by the shoulders, I turned the sweatshirt around so she could see the design. Sarah gasped and covered her mouth with her hand.

"Thanks," I said. "I'm gonna need something warm."

"You'll like Washington. Seattle's a first-rate city. First rate." The astronaut pulled out his wallet and withdrew a business card. "Now, call collect any time you need anything. I've also put the phone numbers of your aunts and uncles on the back. They'll be happy to help you with whatever you need."

Thanks," I said again.

"You've checked your spare tire?"

"Yes."

"Call me from the road if you run into any problems," the astronaut instructed as he circled the car.

"Okay."

He stood next to me now. "College should be the time of your life. Make the most of it."

I got in the car and pulled out of the driveway. In my rearview mirror I saw Sarah returning to the house. The astronaut was still standing in the driveway, following my progress down the street. I glanced down at the sweatshirt. This was one gift I was sure the astronaut had picked out, not just purchased. Neither my sister, nor my mother, would have chosen this one. Underneath a fierce-looking husky, the University of Washington mascot, were the purple-stitched letters that reflected the abbreviation commonly used within the state for the name of the school—U DUB.

Yakima / Seattle,
Summer After Senior Year

"You get away from there, boy!" The voice was angry and authoritative. I figured it must be a cop. "What in the hell are you doing, anyway?" I turned directly into the glare of a flashlight.

"Painting."

"Don't you kids ever get tired of vandalizing public property?"

I assumed the question was rhetorical. I mean, what would be the correct answer to that? Ignoring the trooper, I turned back around and faced the Yakima Valley. The huge hills that surrounded the town were barren and treeless, the Cascades preventing all but the most dogged rain clouds from entering eastern Washington. Below me, the lights of the city twinkled. They thinned as neighborhoods turned into orchards and farmhouses. I could see the white water reflection of the Yakima River where highway lights illuminated bridges. A stiff wind kept blowing my bangs down into my eyes; it smelled of apples and dust. The crunching of boots on gravel approached the spot where I was kneeling. I appraised my handiwork. The law had come too late this time. I was finished. The beam of the flashlight moved across the fresh paint I had applied over faded, peeling original lettering.

"Birthplace of Alan York."

The trooper could read.

"I'll be damned. If this don't puzzle the shit out of me." He clicked off his flashlight and knelt beside me. "What are you? Some kind of good Samaritan? Next are you gonna go down in the valley and fix some of the traffic lights? My squad car here needs a good waxing."

I turned and faced him, but I had nothing to say.

"Who is Alan York, anyway?" he asked.

• • •

The next day I checked into Lander Hall. A sheet of notebook paper was taped to the door of my dorm room. Boyd, Norman/York, Steven was written in black felt tip. I went inside. Norman wasn't there, but the bottom bunk had been made, the desk nearest the window was claimed, and a Cindy Crawford poster was up next to the mirror by the sink. I set my computer on the free desk and threw my suitcase into the empty closet. I walked down the hallway to the pay phone I had passed on my way up.

Sarah answered the phone.

"Hey, this is Steve. Is Dad there?"

Sarah didn't answer immediately. "He isn't home from work yet."

"Just tell him I made it. Tell him I'm safe and sound."